Miguel Alemán Velasco

Copilli

AZTEC PRINCE

DOUBLEDAY & CO., INC.
GARDEN CITY, NEW YORK
1984

Library of Congress Cataloging in Publication Data

Alemán Velasco, Miguel
   Copilli, Aztec prince.

   Translation of: Copilli, corona real.
   I. Title.
PQ7297.A488C613   1984   863

ISBN: 0-385-18901-X
Library of Congress Catalog Number: 83–45010
Published by Editorial Diana, S.A., © 1981
English Translation Copyright © 1984 Doubleday & Company, Inc.
Printed in the United States of America
First Edition

Publisher's Foreword

IN A PROLOGUE to the Mexican edition of *Copilli, Aztec Prince,* the critic Andrés Henestrosa calls the book a "novel, historical narrative and autobiography combined." It is an apt description of this bizarre but captivating, literally other-worldly tale of the triumphs and travails of a young Aztec nobleman.

It was not easy for a youth in the ancient Mexican capital of Tenochtitlán, growing up under the pressures of rigorous training and fierce competition in the many arts, warfare among them, and subject to the stern and often capricious will of a vast pantheon of gods and goddesses.

With its panoply of kings and maidens, knights and retainers, vows, quests, magic and its own exotic variety of chivalry, this story might evoke echoes of King Arthur and the Round Table.

There is, however, a great difference in the sagas: the Arthurian legend, its dim Celtic basis notwithstanding, has always been only a story—magnificent, but a fiction. Whereas the elements of Copilli's tale, including particularly the supernatural, were as real as rock to the millions of souls in the Nahua dominions. And in truth, to Aztec descendants of not many years ago those traditions, those gods and their dire influence, were still all too real.

In his preface the author, Miguel Alemán Velasco, tells us that, researching some incunabula in a Florentine library, he came across an ancient Aztec codex, which with his knowledge of paleography and the Nahua language, he was able to translate as this story of the Prince Copilli.

Now, it must be remembered that those long-ago Mexicans had no written language. Their writing was more illustration —a pictographic system both figurative and phonetic; that is, small drawings, some representing physical objects and others representing vocal sounds. This kind of illustrative message also constituted the low-relief sculpture on public monuments, such as was made miraculously to appear on Copilli's pyramid herein.

The priests of the Conquest, finding many of the Nahua "books" to contain what they considered heretical superstition, had most of them seized and burned. A number survived, however, including some magnificent examples of codices now preserved in great libraries. The priests partially redeemed themselves for this loss to scholarship by indefatigable labors toward preserving at least some part of the Nahua history. They taught the Spanish language to intelligent native scribes and encouraged them to set down Náhuatl terms in Latin letters. Thus appeared chronicles of Aztec life and beliefs in the "confusing but charming mixture of Spanish and Náhuatl" that Miguel Alemán Velasco describes in his preface.

There is yet another great difference between the Arthurian and the Aztec legends. Though bloody battles, dragons, treachery, death were indeed a grim part of the former, the Thomas Malory and particularly the Tennyson version have bequeathed us a vision of Camelot as suffused with gentleness, romance, fidelity and tender love. To the Anglo mind, on the other hand, the Aztec world is violence, human sacrifices, preoccupation with death and a positive wallowing in blood.

Life was indeed violent in early Mexico. *Nature* was violent, visiting upon a helpless population earthquake, fire, flood and famine in perpetual succession, each seeming to threaten the very end of the world. Obviously only the most powerful dieties could prevail and protect against such cataclysms. And to propitiate divinities of such eminence required the supreme offering, the sacrifice of life. At times the supply of candidates for these honors was perilously close to exhaustion and ritual wars had to be undertaken against neighboring dominions to replenish the stock.

"Clearly, it is difficult for us to come to a true understanding of what human sacrifice meant to the sixteenth century Aztec," observed the distinguished authority Jacques Soustelle; "but it may be observed that every culture possesses its own idea of what is and what is not cruel. At the height of their career the Romans shed more blood in their circuses and for their amusement than ever the Aztecs did before their idols. The Spaniards, so sincerely moved by the cruelty of the native priests, nevertheless massacred, burnt, mutilated and tortured with a perfectly clear conscience. We, who shudder at the tale of the bloody rites of ancient Mexico, have seen with our own eyes and in our own days civilised nations proceed systematically to the extermination of millions of human beings and to the perfection of weapons capable of annihilating in one second a hundred times more victims than the Aztecs ever sacrificed."*

In any case, death was regarded wholly differently by these peoples than by later civilizations. "Death and life are no more than two sides of the same reality . . . no people in history have been so much haunted by the grim presence of death as the Mexicans; but for them life came out of death, as the young plant comes from the mouldering seed in the earth."†

WE KNOW, of course, that Miguel Alemán Velasco did not really discover the record of Prince Copilli in a Florentine codex: this is after all a novel. But with the exception of the prince himself and the dialogue which Alemán acknowledges adding, that record does indeed exist in the ancient codices spared by the Conquest. The Aztec world as depicted herein is an authentic record, skillfully assembled by the author, who, as Andrés Henestrosa said, "is an expert in the ancient history of Mexico, with ample knowledge of its mythology and of one of the richest . . . languages spoken in ancient Anáhuac."

Señor Henestrosa continued, "*Copilli, Aztec Prince* is the timeless story of a moment in Mexico which is as much present as past; of a reign, a government; of certain men, of a family with a deeply-rooted national identity. It has validity today: by merely changing names and situations and adding a few details, it would depict the same reality as that of a thousand years ago. For the Mexico of yesterday lives in the Mexico of today; we cannot understand the present apart from our remote origins."

The same reality indeed: it does not take a political expert to see the parallel between the conventions of changing the

* *The Daily Life of the Aztecs* (New York: Macmillan, 1962).
† Ibid.

ruler in Copilli's day and that of the presidential succession in modern Mexico, a parallel particularly evident in Chapter XII herein.

In addition to our appreciation of Señor Henestrosa's comments, we should like to acknowledge here the contribution made by Sharon Washtien Franco and Catherine Steele, who did the original basic translation, and by Walter I. Bradbury, who contributed further translation and editing for the United States edition.

Preface

I HAVE ALWAYS BEEN a profound admirer of the history and primitive legends of Mexico. I am of the opinion that we Mexicans are not aware of the fabulous wealth which we have in the deeds, customs and legacies of the peoples who formerly inhabited our land, which today, through absurd misfortune, has been reduced to half its original size.

I am forever searching in libraries and public and private archives for information which might throw some light on the history of Mexico previous to its contact with the West, and one day, going through incunabula in a Florentine library, I came across a scroll of old *maguey* papers, that is, papers made in the ancient manner from the maguey cactus. They contained drawings and writing done in a confusing but charming mixture of Spanish and Náhuatl, the language of the Aztecs.

The central figure of the story—the hieroglyphic is repeated on every page—is a young prince dressed in splendid garments and wearing on his black hair the crown of an Aztec lord. The *tzin,* or symbol, of the royal family is detached in the drawing, indicating that the prince never occupied the throne of his ancestors. This kind of codex goes back to the last years of reign of the people who called themselves *Mexica.*

From my knowledge of paleography I was able to establish that the finding dated back to the end of the sixteenth century, and that the *tlacuilo,* or narrator, must have been a Christianized Indian who knew Spanish. The abundance of ancient citations and primitive legends clearly indicates that the story was dictated to him by an old chieftain, for a young man born at a time when Spain was already mistress of half of Anáhuac, the lake area of Mexico's central valley, could not otherwise have been familiar with such lore.

The meticulous presentation of ideas, reflecting the Nahua style, repeated in hierolgyphics, and the care with which the colors were used in the painting of certain images were the first indications that I had definitely come across a prominent Mexica of unknown name. After briefly consulting the key books on Mexican archaeology, I was able to decipher the prince's symbol. It appears in many other Aztec representations next to kings or nobles: the symbol of the tiara or royal crown. But in this case, since the symbol was not accompanied by any other figure (such as the descending eagle in the case of the Emperor Cuauhtémoc), I deduced that its repetition meant rather that it was the young lord's own name, bestowed with respect to a special rank. Later, after reading the rest of the chronicle, I was able to confirm my assumption.

The events recorded in the document constitute the life, reflections, doctrine and predictions of a young son of the historical ruler Axayácatl. In the course of the narration the hero refers to this Aztec king as "my father" or "my lord," although considering that Axayácatl reigned from 1469 to 1482, the chronology is confusing. The confusion may possibly be due to errors made by the instigator of the codex, or to imprecision by the scribe. In any event, I am obliged to limit myself to simply transcribing the text, so that the reader may draw his own conclusions.

The prince's name, then, is Royal Crown, which in Aztec is *Copilli.*

THE NATURAL YEAR begins when the new grass springs up in the fields, which retain their verdure until winter, when the grass withers and dies. With the passing of the cold the earth reclothes itself with shoots, the new growth marking a natural year. It is *xíhuitl,* the new grass, that counts the passing years and measures the sun's course for the return of green to the ground. At that time the year was known as the *xíhuitl* and has retained that name up to the present day, there being no other term corresponding to "year" in the Náhuatl language. The cycle, repeated with the passing of each year, follows the invariable order, the regulated movement of the stars which gives rise to the diversity of seasons, weather and products of the land. Thus it was that the Aztecs began to devote themselves to the study of the firmament, especially the sun and the moon, which, because of their size, lent themselves to the observation of their mysterious movements.

The Aztecs arranged their year around the moon, whose daily mutations made its revolution more perceptible. The year was apportioned into "new moon" periods of twenty-six days, each divided into two thirteen-day parts. They began to count the first part on the day in which the moon appeared in the sky, and it was called *mextozoliztli,* the wake of the moon. When the thirteen days had passed, they began to count the second part, known as the *mecochiliztli,* the slumber of the moon.

I find no authority for how many of these new-moon periods constituted the Aztec year. There is no doubt that they were used as months and that even after the calendar was corrected, the month was called *metztli*—moon. On the basis of their erudite estimations they continued to count the days in units of thirteen, maintaining, under a different form, the new-moon division which they had used in the beginning. Some authors believe that in those days they numbered the years by olympiads, that is, by units of four, indicated by four hieroglyphs, or symbols of elements later used in their calculations. This hypothesis seems probable, at least for the period previous to the correction and regulation; later on they began to measure time in units of six years. We cannot establish with any certainty or precision the kind of system they used or how far their knowledge had advanced when the correction was made. We are told, however, that nine centuries after the hurricanes, the year was indicated by the hieroglyph of a flint—*cetécpatl*—which according to the tables would appear to have been the year 3945 of the world.

AND SO, one afternoon last autumn, chance led me to the ancient scroll. From the outset I was filled with the profound, ineffable spirit of the story; I felt my life as a researcher to be linked in some way to that of the unknown Copilli, whom the codex describes as a bold and passionate knight, and a philosopher given to politics.

The constant intervention of the Aztec gods in the tale, whose literary form I have modified by recourse to dialogue, evokes the transcendental movement of the Nahua epic, which, like the Greek, frequently transforms its champions into gods or heroes and puts certain concepts into the mouths of divinities to suggest eternal verities.

The few obvious inconsistencies in the story are very probably due to the scribes, or *tlacuilos,* who adapted the manuscript for the edification of future generations. My folio is clearly only one of the last copies of the magnificent text.

The final part of the Copilli codex was undoubtedly written by a different person. Its Indian characteristics are very much in evidence. It does not form part of the original document and limits itself to narrating—with great esthetic verve and a certain primitive realism—the fulfillment of the prince's desires. This postscript I have left virtually intact; unlike the main body of the work, it presents no problems for the lay reader.

The impressive pyramid around which the story evolves is said to be situated in the area of Teotihuacán, site of the famous ruins, near Mexico City. However, precise data have been neither confirmed nor corrected by the experts. One gathers from a reference made in the codex that the figure of the unknown warrior found in the central part of one of the frescoes in Tepantitlán may be that of Prince Copilli. Of course, until this assumption, like that of the pyramid, is scientifically verified, it will remain within the realm of imagination rather than reality.

MIGUEL ALEMÁN VELASCO

I

The Pyramid

SOME SEVENTY KILOMETERS up the valley of Anáhuac lies the ancient dead city of Teotihuacán—"place of the gods." There it was that Copilli, son of the late emperor Axayácatl, with the assistance of a group of master builders and priests, was raising up a pyramid. It was a structure of four terraces, of which the face of the third level, recently completed, was decorated with magnificent hieroglyphs. The base and first level were to be adorned later. Work had been started on the fourth section and was proceeding feverishly until the arrival of hurricane rains so violent that the slaves and overseers were forced to stop all activity.

The pyramid was laid out in an east-westerly direction in accordance with the movement of the sun; on its truncated top the men were beginning to erect an incense burner of purest gold resting on the head of Quetzalcóatl, the plumed serpent. The god's statue must not cast the slightest shadow during the days on which the sun reached its zenith. On the north face of the pyramid a central staircase led up to the imposing figure. On the southern side was a feature which distinguished this pyramid from all others: an arched cavity giving access to a chamber one hundred meters long and equally wide, vaulted by five arches supported by sloping slabs bracing the keystone. The arches divided the chamber into five sections: a kind of living room, a dining room, a private bedchamber, another room with several beds and a kind of kitchen. Through the main bedroom flowed an underground stream connecting the second bedroom with the kitchen. The latter was served by a small garden, its bed warmed by the sun's rays filtering down through one of the eyes of Quetzalcóatl. Here there were strange instruments of smooth minerals, gleaming like mirrors. This offered Copilli's only communication with outside, directed toward the Sun. The god Huitzilopochtli and Coyolxauhqui, the Moon, acted as intermediaries between the interior and exterior of the pyramid. In the main part of the soberly decorated living room was an obsidian replica of the Aztec calendar which reflected, night and day, the light of ceremonial torches in the foreground. It was like a library, filled with codices and engraved stone tablets containing great wisdom.

The walls were hung with tapestries—*chalchiuhpétlatl,* meaning worked with emeralds, and *teocuitlapétlat,* woven with gold —and these highlighted floors covered with feather rugs, called *quetzalpétlat.* In the *inezahualcalli,* the area for fasting and penance, which communicated with the dining room, was a small altar dedicated to King Axayácatl and bearing the symbol of friendship: two clasped hands. The principal bedroom was dominated by an image of the god Tláloc with outstretched arms, unique of its kind, and especially commissioned by Copilli.

Prince Copilli had not yet set foot on the pyramid, nor did the artisans and architects, on their part, know the reason for the construction of the immense building.

The pyramid was situated at approximately one kilometer from the Pyramid of the Moon, for Copilli worshipped Coyolxauhqui. It was surrounded by smaller elevations separated by large open squares intended for worship. The patios and platforms were framed by the walls of the buildings, these sacred areas forming units conceived with grandiose structural uniformity and following a meticulous plan whose central axis comprised the great open spaces used for religious ceremonies and gatherings of the faithful; the shrine itself was the virtual center and the crowning splendor. In the area of Teotihuacán Copilli's majestic pyramid was the highest after those dedicated to the Sun and Moon respectively.

The rain was getting fiercer. It was physically impossible for work to go on. Copilli's attendants bore him on a litter to a cave near the central pyramid; there they waited patiently for three days and three nights, until they exhausted the provisions which *tamemes*, bearers, had brought from the nearby settlement of Acolman. The rain cut off fresh supplies and put an end to the dancing which had accompanied the construction of the pyramid. An atmosphere of melancholy gradually pervaded the scene.

Now Xólotl—he of the large eyes—approached Copilli, who at that moment was peering out at the sky through one of the openings in the cave.

"Lord," he said, "well you know that in this city, uninhabited for many centuries, we have no means of obtaining sustenance from either land or sky. The very lizards have gone into hiding and neither our stones nor our arrows can reach them.

The bats have reduced the number of our craftsmen and an epidemic is threatening. The waters have risen to a great height and are beginning to gush into the cave. Yet again the gods are trying to prevent the construction of the pyramid.

"Abandon your plan, lord," he continued, "and let us return to Tenochtitlán where you are loved and needed by your father's friends. Moreover, your father is dead—your sacrifice is no longer necessary—Moctezuma can rescue you. . . ."

"Don't go on, Xólotl," Copilli replied. "My resolve to build this shrine is stronger than I myself. I shall never cease in my endeavors to complete it, for Quetzalcóatl has written that it must be so. I have determined to call upon Tláloc, god of wind and rain, for surely Tezcatlipoca has turned against me once more."

Thereupon Prince Copilli wrapped himself in a white *áyatl*, richly adorned with the blue and black motif denoting his rank. On his shoulder gleamed the face of the god Tonatiuh. Then, swift as an arrow, he disappeared through the cave entrance, his followers watching in amazement as he snatched the helmet of the order from the hands of a tiger knight and placed it on his head.

Swiftly he reached the citadel wall, where he bounded up the steps like one inspired. Turning onto the Avenue of the Dead, he raced toward the courtyard of the temple of Tláloc.

The rain continued to fall in torrents, outlining Copilli's muscular figure beneath the *áyatl*. The prince seemed now to emerge, now to disappear, as he sped across the ancestral stones. Thunderbolts accompanied the regal runner like a battle charge—or a funeral cortege. He was going to see Tláloc, the mysterious deity of wind and rain who had dominated Copilli's soul since he was a small child.

The venerable monarch, his father, had said to him, "Tláloc protects you; go to him whenever you are in doubt or in need . . . The good god has never abandoned the house of our ancestors."

Now on this third night of the hurricane the words of his progenitor drummed in his mind. Before his rain-lashed eyes the image of the lord of hurricanes, germinator and destroyer, seemed to appear intermittently, surrounded by *tlaloques*, the minor gods who regulate the winds and rains from the infernal mansion of the East, the Tlalocán, place of lush vegetation where the drowned come together at the god's command.

Gradually out of the foggy wetness the mud-covered walls of the temple loomed into sight. A sudden flash of lightning illuminated the jeweled eyes of the tiger helmet. Through the mist Copilli made out the rough opening which served as an entrance to the abode of Tláloc. Night sounds could be heard reverberating within. For an instant they evoked the *huéhuetles*, the great drums of the priests in the ceremony of the new fire, as Copilli slipped inside the temple.

His chilled body tensed like a tree in a storm, the young prince proceeded into the great columned hall. Regally he shook off the rain and divested himself of his *áyatl.* He dropped his helmet and only his *maxtlatl*, breechclout, covered his sculpted thighs. His hair flowing loose, his gaze lost in the shadowy depths of the shrine, he kneeled in homage. Beneath his knees the earth seemed to resound with the subterranean moan of the gale savaging the sacred city. Suddenly he paused, as if searching for something, and proceeded to tear thorns from the dry leaves of a maguey plant growing inside the temple. With the thorns he pierced his eyelids, ears and hands, without the slightest grimace of pain.

"Now Tláloc must know," reflected the prince in an ambivalent transport of reverence and boldness, "whether or not I am worthy to enter his house and be brought into his presence—I have wounded my hands that I may not touch any part of his abode, my ears, that I may hear nothing, my eyes, that I may not contemplate the exquisite image of the goddess Xochiquétzal, half flower, half woman, who lives in Tamoanchán, and who was carried away by my mortal enemy Yáotl, behind whose mask hides Tezcatlipoca. . . ."

He found before him a cup and drank of its contents, agave juice mixed with *toloache,* and, enraptured, fell into a swoon.

After a time the light came back to his eyes, and he felt an ethereal floating sensation. Now all was clear: the door of Tamoanchán and the dwelling place of Tláloc had simultaneously opened for him.

He found himself in a great palace comprising five enormous rooms, like those of his own pyramid; in the center there was a patio, and there, four colossal pools of tranquil water. The pool nearest to him contained the rains that fall in their appointed season, fertilizing the earth so that it gives forth bounteous fruits; the second, the water which forms rain clouds over the harvests and destroys the produce; the third, the water which freezes and dries up the plants; and the final pool, the water which rots and renders sterile all it falls upon.

From the rooms the many ministers of Tláloc emerged to receive Copilli. These were small, almost dwarflike figures, with skins of many colors: blue, purple, white—even yellow and red. They dwell in this place, carrying in their hands enormous water pitchers and great sticks. When the supreme rain god gives the command, it is they who, indifferently, water the earth with the huge sprinklers which they carry. When thunder roars, it is they smashing the pitchers with their sticks, and flinging the broken fragments to the ground, filling the night with the terrifying din of thunderbolts.

With ceremonial humility, Copilli permitted himself to be escorted to the fifth chamber by one of the ministers. At the far end of the room, seated on an aquamarine *icpalli*, were Tláloc and Chalchiutlicue, goddess of springs and flowing waters. Around them were children ankle-deep in water, frolicking and splashing the luxurious garments of Tláloc's warriors. The scene was framed in a water mirror in the center of the room. The wall at the end of the hall was covered by a curtain of water, resembling infinite sparkling jets of gold dust and obsidian. In his left hand Tláloc held a thunderbolt and in his right he bore a shield, the upper part representing fertility, the lower part, sterility. A mask covered the god's face; his huge single eye, like the full moon, gazed at Copilli.

The latter kneeled before the celestial couple and kissed Tláloc's blue sandals.

Interrupting the prince's reverence, the god spoke.

"Friend Copilli, chosen by the gods, some important matter must have brought you to me, something which you cannot resolve alone. Your father, Axayácatl, consecrated you to me. Lately in Tamoanchán I have received his prayers, from the twelfth sky, where he expresses anxiety for your person."

"O Tláloc, lord of thunder and lightning," replied the supplicant, "your ministers have broken their water pitchers on Teotihuacán and prevented the completion of my work, a splendid pyramid which I am building in the center of the Sacred City."

"And to what purpose does Copilli set his slaves to the arduous task of such a construction?"

"Forgive me, lord of the waters, son of Tonacatecutli and Tonacacíhuatl," Copilli begged, "but I cannot divulge to you the reason for my endeavor, for fear that it reach the ears of Tezcatlipoca, your brother, and Mictlantecutli, lord of hell, who, I assure you, would prevent me at any cost from accomplishing my project. At this moment they do not know the purpose of my pyramid and so they do not seek to destroy it."

Copilli paused, then added earnestly, "However, I can tell you that I have little time left to complete its construction."

"Illustrious prince, son of mortals," said Tláloc, "I respect the righteous zeal which burns in your cheeks. This iron will which yields to nothing is a quality of the gods rather than of men. And since you have begun construction on a work in which you rejoice, it is well that you go on and see it finished. Let not Coyolxauhqui's shadows swallow up forever what you hope to be the ripened fruit of your labor.

"And to confirm my resolution to help you," continued the god, "know that I will accompany you forthwith to the shadow of the *pirul* trees of Teotihuacán, and will follow you to the center of the valley, that I may admire your mysterious pyramid and ease the effects of the celestial furies. But I remind you—now that your father is dead, you have no need to carry out your project. . . ."

And addressing the *tlaloques:* "And you, careless ministers of my cult and lineage, cease beating the *teponaxtlis* of thunder and lightning, reassemble the fragments of the mystic pitchers and fill them with the tears of Chalchiutlicue, the waters which flood the fields and rot the *centli.* Let Tonatiuh, the Sun, shine and dry the maize and let the four hundred rabbits of abundance scatter among the magueys and *quelites;* let Chicomecóatl, goddess of the seven serpents, crawl through holes and drink the water from the pools, and kill the poisonous darkness of the toads; let Ehécatl, the wind, cease blowing through the orifices of the flutes, and let the sea conch carry back to the clouds the sounds of Tláloc's peace. May the green and blue, indigo and emerald descend once more to Copilli's site and spur the construction of his pyramid. . . ."

Cowed by the god's speech, the *tlaloques* hastened to obey; they slaked the thirst of the springs, collected the scattered clay fragments and dried up the sluggish pools which drown the pulp of the magueys and leave no room for Tochli, the rabbit, to lavish the abundance which is his symbol.

Again Copilli was overcome by drowsiness. His smooth body seemed to become finer and more yielding: his senses were a hummingbird nestling its head in a soft hollow nest. At his side he saw the mighty Tláloc, the wrathful gaze of his single moon-eye softened. He seemed to sense among his dreams the ultimate breath of Xochiquétzal, playing a *huéhuetl* of mystical sound.

Now the prince, again awake, shuddered with the icy cold. The temple stones had the whiteness of the snowcapped volcano, Ixtaccíhuatl. Through the blood streaming from his eyelids he could see the great Tláloc observing him, his expression at once ominous and tender, clouded in mystery.

"You alone can see me, noble lord," the god intoned. "Lead me, then, to the threshold of your pyramid." And immersing his hands in the *xicapoyas*—sacred water springs— he tenderly bathed Copilli's wounds, healing them.

At the very moment god and prince left the temple and walked through the dawn shadows, an enormous rainbow appeared above Teotihuacán's great Pyramid of the Sun, symbolizing the alliance of Tláloc and Copilli.

The song of the *zenzontles* accompanied the strange pair to the cave where the prince's attendants were sleeping. Xólotl alone awaited his master, keeping vigil over the shield and mace, his bow drawn in readiness.

"Your Highness, lord Copilli," said Xólotl, "where have you been? In vain we searched for you in the storm, with torches and candles . . . Did you not hear your friends and slaves bewailing you?"

"Rejoice, faithful Xólotl," replied the prince, "for Tláloc himself, whom you see here at my right hand, has ordered the heavens to clear and to cover our work with their benevolent influence."

Xólotl stared. "Noble lord, you rave," he protested. "Perhaps the malign spirit of Tezcatlipoca has entered your body and filled you with evil humors. Or the rain germs have assailed your throat and lips and distorted the meaning of your wise words. . . ."

Then Copilli remembered that only he could see the god. Smiling, he asked his friend to bring him a fresh *áyatl.* Then, turning back to the lord of the rains, he said, "Let us proceed, powerful *tecuhtli;* you will do my palace great honor by your visit. . . ."

In mute amazement Xólotl followed his master and the invisible Tláloc to the foot of Copilli's pyramid. There they halted, and Copilli, with a sweeping gesture that seemed to embrace the entire horizon, addressed Tláloc. "Behold, deity of thunder and cyclones, the palace I am building. Let me explain why thousands of slaves are laboring under the most difficult conditions to erect this monument.

"Despite my youth, I have lived in three reigns over the Anáhuac valley, and have known betrayal and friendship, honesty and intrigue, love and hate, power and justice. As a child,

I saw upraised the glittering maces of avengers and the arrows of assailants and betrayers flying over my head.

"I have seen blood. I have witnessed the benevolence and power of my father, the just Axayácatl, trampled underfoot by those who used him as a stepping-stone to personal glory . . . I have learned well, if I may be permitted to say so, the science of statehood and the politics of the realm, and I wish, O god, to advise my contemporaries and all mankind so that with the passing of winter suns, they may in time concur in what must be done and what avoided to retain the power, to control the malcontents and enemies, rewarding faithful servants and aggrandizing the land with conquests and prosperity. To receive that absolute power it is necessary to die at the hand of the successor, *huey tecuhtli,* the new supreme lord, in the rite of Huitzilopochtli.

"The two upper terraces of the pyramid I dedicate to history and the prophecies which Quetzalcóatl inspired in me through the whispering evening wind," continued the prince. "In them is condensed my life experience and a lust for the struggle, captured there as our forebear, the doomed Emperor Chimalpopoca, was imprisoned in his sacrificial cage." Copilli paused. "But there is something I lack, Lord," he went on. "Something which my youth and the tales of my ancestors are barely able to trace: the unfolding of the events which preceded the last two eras. Without this history, the base of my monument and the first terrace will remain empty and useless, and for many the narration contained in the two subsequent terraces will be meaningless. . . .

"Tláloc, powerful master, I require from you a second favor: I beseech you to take upon your powerful shoulders the burden of this story: chew the enchanted herbs of the earth, *toloache,* and the magic mushrooms; dazzle my senses with a sparkling cascade of memories. Tell me, what happened before Mixcóatl hunted his first venison? When did the breeze first sway the *ácatl* of our earliest ancestors, and why was the green serpent of the prickly *tenochoca* pear devoured by Cuauhtli, to whose order of warriors I belong? The cosmic origin of all that exists is for me a secret greater than the shadows which fall on the *teocallis* of my town, always at the same hour and on the same day of the year, save for every fourth year. With the sure wisdom of your divine eloquence, enlighten your helpless adopted son. Inscribe for me the history of the world on the first two terraces of my pyramid, that I may better understand the story of my people."

"For you," replied Tláloc, "it will be done."

And with a flourish of lightning and miraculous water jets, hieroglyphics multiplied on the base and first section of the pyramid's bronzelike stone. Copilli felt as though he had awakened from one nightmare only to enter another. Then it was finished. Copilli, enraptured, contemplated the magic gift of his thunderous protector.

Suddenly he realized that Tláloc was no longer at his side.

II
The Inscriptions

WHETHER BY TLÁLOC'S COMMAND or not, from behind the pyramid now appeared Moxotli, the scribe, as he was wont to do, for at that time he was entrusted with transcribing all important events of the Anáhuac valley in codices highly prized by the Aztec nobility.

"Noble lord," he addressed the prince, "I will relate in few words what is written on the first two terraces of your pyramid, inscribed for you there by some mysterious hand, as it was not even imagined one moon ago.

"In the beginning, there was nothing and from nothing Tonacatecuhtli and Tonacacíhuatl were created. They dwelt in what is now the thirteenth sky, built by their own command, and later they created many other celestial mansions where they might live more comfortably. In the night of time, as it is told, they had four sons: Tlatlauhqui Tezcatlipoca, the red one; Yayauhqui Tezcatlipoca, the black one; Quetzalcóatl and Huitzilopochtli, and one daughter, Coyolxauhqui; she was quartered by her brother Huitzilopochtli, who tore out her heart and rolled her down the Hill of the Snake. Since then it has become known that for six hundred years the gods remained at rest until the four sons met to determine what they must do. The firstborn—Tezcatlipoca the red—argued against the resolutions which were being discussed.

" 'Our brother Quetzalcóatl, who has from the first held one of the highest celestial ranks, now wants to usurp our father's *icpalli*. This can never be the goal of life.'

"Like his brother, Tezcatlipoca the black was also opposed to Quetzalcóatl's thoughts of rebellion. Then Huitzilopochtli, the most wicked and cunning of the four, went secretly, in silence, to his father.

"Defying the paternal power, Tezcatlipoca the black boldly seated himself upon the throne of Tonacatecuhtli and mustered several eagle knights. His first command was that Quetzalcóatl be killed. But the wise, skillful warrior Quetzalcóatl killed the retainers around his infernal brother, seized him by the throat and hurled him from the throne. Tezcatlipoca was caught by Tonacatecuhtli, who cast him from the thirteenth sky amid thunder and lightning, ordering him to disappear into the darkness of the night. And thus was settled the succession to the *icpalli*, for the benefit of Anáhuac."

Moxotli continued the narration, to Copilli's rapt attention.

"Quetzalcóatl and Huitzilopochtli remain in control. They determine and carry out the tasks of creation. Quetzalcóatl first fashions a half sun that gives little light; Huitzilopochtli creates fire. Then, united once more, the three loyal sons bring forth water—*atl*—naming Tláloc and his consort Chalchiutlicue to be its masters. And finally they form a huge fish in the waters, which will always be of great import to your people, O Copilli, because all troubles will be born of it and to it they will return. This fish—*cipactli*—became the Earth with its god Tlaltecuhtli. Everything that he creates will come to an end someday, he himself devouring it all.

"Quetzalcóatl's half sun sheds little light; it has to be completed. So Tezcatlipoca the red becomes the Sun and so remains for six hundred and seventy-six years, when Quetzalcóatl, with a blow of his staff, knocks him into the water and transforms himself, in turn, into Tonatiuh, the luminous-star king. Tlalocantecuhtli takes the place of the sun.

"Then Quetzalcóatl, in the form of a man, comes from Chicomóstoc, site of the seven caves. Modest and temperate, as is told, he begins by doing penance in order to preach the laws of nature. He introduces fasting, unknown in those domains. The sacrifice of bleeding ears and tongue he conscientiously practices in order to fend off the demon who seduces hearing and speech with improper temptations. He allows no sacrifices of human or animal blood; his offerings are of bread and roses and other flowers, of perfume and of colors. With wondrous effectiveness, he prohibits war, robbery and killing, eliminating all the afflictions mortals visit on one another.

"Then one evil day," Moxotli narrated, "Tezcatlipoca decided with perverse cunning to abandon the region. 'I will make *teómetl*—*pulque*—and have him drink of it. He will take leave of his senses and will do no more penance.' Tezcatlipoca muses, 'I will say that I am going to give him a new body, for he dare not appear before his people with the one he has now.' With this he seizes a double obsidian mirror and wraps it up.

"Tezcatlipoca disguises himself in the mask of Yáotl the jester and goes to Quetzalcóatl's palace. He says to the pages guarding the entrance, 'Go tell the priest that I have come to show him his body and to give him a new one.'

"The pages go in search of Quetzalcóatl, who can hear them, though he is hidden from their eyes. He asks them, 'Who is that, that dares to disturb the high priest in such a manner?'

" 'He's a worthy man,' the pages answer, 'quite amusing, and one who does your people many good services.'

"The disguised Tezcatlipoca is admitted, and Quetzalcóatl greets him. 'Welcome, old man,' he says. 'Where have you come from? What do you mean about showing me my body? Tell me. . . .'

" 'I am your vassal,' Tezcatlipoca replies, 'and I come from the foothills of Popocatépetl. Observe, my lord, your body . . .' He holds out the mirror. 'See, and know yourself.'

"Taking the gift, Quetzalcóatl looks at his reflection. Perturbed by what he sees, he exclaims, 'I imagined but never really believed that I was a *huehue*—an old man—so worn.' Trembling, he rises to his feet to show himself to better advantage in the obsidian mirror.

" 'You see, old man?' insists Tezcatlipoca. 'Now you know why your people no longer respect or fear you—why they laugh at you rather than admire you. How can they follow your counsel if you deliver it from your bed in this room where you hide from the eyes of your very attendants?'

" 'What can I do? There is much more that I must teach, but with my body as it is . . .' Quetzalcóatl strives to explain.

" 'That's why I have come, old man,' interrupts the false Yáotl. 'Drink from this jug and you will become sound.'

" 'What is this drink you offer that I may be cured?' asks Quetzalcóatl naively.

" 'The water that cures and renews all, the water that will make you powerful. I drew it from the *xicapoyas* of the Great Temple, but as you never go to the *teocalli*, it is most likely that you do not know it. It is called *teómetl* and is the drink of the gods.'

" 'Let me drink of it,' urges Quetzalcóatl, persuaded by the seductive voice of Tezcatlipoca, hiding behind the mask of Yáotl the jester. And he drinks deeply, until he feels his strength returning and himself more godlike, though in fact he is descending to the opposite, human, condition. Then the false Yáotl paints Quetzalcóatl's body green; adorns him with varicolored plumes, crowns him with a helmet resembling a serpent's head and gives him a voice strong and low. Finally he covers his body with a cape of precious stones and feathers. At Yáotl's urging, Quetzalcóatl regards his reflection in the mirror once more.

"He finds himself truly imposing.

"Now," continued Moxotli, "under the influence of the brew, Quetzalcóatl goes outside before sunset. His drunken state shocks and dismays his followers. What Tezcatlipoca had told him has proved true: now they do not just respect him—they fear him. He is endowed with great power. They worship him. He is a god.

"For some time after the sunset ceremonies he continues to drink the fatal potion, in the company of his new friend, until he takes leave of his senses. Then 'Yáotl' bears him upon his shoulders to the outskirts of the city, followed by Quetzalcóatl's thirteen disciples, who, save one, never abandon him.

"The following day, when the god regained consciousness, 'Yáotl' gives him more *teómetl* so he will forget what has happened. Then he counsels him to leave the Anáhuac valley and make his way to the coast. Still feeling the effects of the *pulque,* the unsuspecting Quetzalcóatl sets off for the shore, accompanied by his disciples. He delights in his great power, evident wherever he goes. He is worshipped as a god, which indeed he is. One day in the year *ce ácatl,* they arrive at the shore, a lovely site called Tlillán Tlapallán. But by now, too late, Quetzalcóatl is beginning to understand why disrespect is growing around him. It is like an enormous poisonous mushroom planted by the deceitful Tezcatlipoca. Attended by his disciples, he bewails his misfortune, there on the rocks which still bear the imprint of his body. Tezcatlipoca has not told him the ultimate secret—the price he must pay for the gift of power. Now he understands.

"He must leave, but before he departs, he gathers his accoutrements and straightens his plumes and his green mask. 'I will return, my children,' he says. 'I will return, not in my present shape but in another form. I will return to punish the false gods, the wicked, those who with seeming friendship have betrayed both thee and me. I am confident that one day the fifth Sun of Tlapallán will shine forth, bringing happiness and prosperity for all Aztecs.' Then he sets himself afire and disappears over the infinite curve of the Aztec ocean.

"There are those who say he ascended in a chariot which had come down from the Sun to carry him back.

"The curse will endure: not one of the lords of Tenochtitlán who holds the great power unlawfully will be pardoned. When their inexorable term is concluded, they must die at the hand of their successor, before Tezcatlipoca's shrine. Thus it will be if they fulfill their appointed duty. If they do not, the parable will not be completed, and they will die at the hands of the populace."

III

The Dominance
of the Empire

AFTER READING the impressive legend of Quetzalcóatl, Moxotli the chronicler went on to read from the second terrace of the pyramid. His eyes devoured the enormous inscriptions, which then seemed to recede among the stones of the edifice as if obeying the divine mandate of the god Tláloc.

"The Aztec race," he read, "under the magic guidance of

Tenoch, came from the tribes of Chicomóstoc, site of the seven caves; there dwelt the ancestors of all present races. But not many years later, lord of Tenochtitlán, the valiant Aztec empire fell under the control of and was forced to render tribute to the Tepanecas of Atzcapotzalco, who hardened their iron rule during the reign of Tezozómoc.

"The empire of the Alcolhuas or Texcocans suffered the same fate as had befallen that of the Aztecs. And many other empires succumbed as well. The just ruler Ixtlilxóchitl, father of Netzahualcóyotl, lost his kingdom and his life. The Alcolhua prince, heir to the throne, had to wander in the mountains and valleys until the time came that he might liberate his people from their slavery.

"But it came to pass, when the mighty warrior Ixcóatl was king of Tenochtitlán, that his soldiers joined with those of Netzahualcóyotl to shake off the rule of their oppressors. The alliance of these two formidable races, with whom the Tlacopanos joined forces as well, marked the creation of a great political triangle—a united force that gradually increased in power, after a bloody and successful revolution that took the lives of many men of the valley.

"When the peace had been concluded, King Ixcóatl devoted himself to extending his borders in all directions. Under his conquering mace, the Chalcas were brought to their knees. The *tobeyos* of the north also fell, as well as the neighboring dominion of Tlaltelolco. It is even said that he vanquished the peoples of Cuauhnáhuac, although this conquest has also been attributed to others.

"But the day came when, in accordance with the perfect design of the gods, the people of Tenochtitlán had to light their funerary censers and burn the *copal* of tears, for the valiant King Ixcóatl had died and his body lay in the grand *teocalli*. Thus were fulfilled the words of Tezcatlipoca.

"I know not," continued the narrator, "in what manner those deeds relate to those which follow. There is great similarity between that turbulent era and that which we are now living through: the monarchs of Anáhuac are firmly establishing their rule and their power is increasingly concentrated in the central plateau.

"One of the realms that merits a place on the panels of your pyramid is that of the Tariácuri king, Tangantzuan Caltzonzín, executioner of the Chichimec king Omeácatl. The head of his monarchy was established in Pátzcuaro. Once this king had taken control of the government, he cast out all the Chichimecas from the lake and from the island of Janitzio. The ceremonies that followed his coronation were strange, different from those hitherto known, notable for their lack of religiosity and pomp.

"He always received the support of his people, to whom he listened daily in his palace. After conquering the remaining islands of the kingdom of Tzintzuntzan, he distributed the property of the former lords to those who previously had had nothing. But the favorable omens that had heralded the beginning of his reign faded without the sovereign's having fulfilled his good intentions. His hopes would have to wait for a time when other rulers would teach the people to love the land and care for it so that it would produce. In various islands of his kingdom a marvelous water of many uses had been found. The neighboring peoples who had settled on those islands had discovered and were exploiting it. They were already familiar with the properties of that dark liquid called *chapópotl,* which did not resemble natural water and produced flames, light and fire.

"*Caltzonzín* means 'absolute monarch.' The Caltzonzín appointed the lords; he chose the most suitable men according to what, in the wisdom of his absolute power, he deemed necessary for the unity of his kingdom and the realization of his goals. His subjects loved him. Multitudes mourned when he withdrew to the sky of Tamoanchán, like all sovereigns executed by their successors. In Tamoanchán only he and his successors could be consulted—that memorable Purépecha king, always quiet and reserved, as becomes a monarch."

IV
The First Moctezuma

MOXOTLI CONTINUED to read the inscriptions. When he came to the reign of the wise Moctezuma, he read:

"When the *tlalocán* with its four electors meet, there is little doubt as to the man whom they think worthy to ascend the throne because of his talent and service to his country. It is Moctezuma Ilhuicamina, son of Huitzilíhuitl, a warrior like his electors. In that battle-filled era it was thought that the leader of armies, the *tlacatécatl,* would also be the best leader of the people. Immediately, as was the custom of the Triple Alliance, the *tecuhtlis,* lords of Acolhuacán, Texcoco and Tlacopán, together with the other chiefs of the neighboring vassalages, are told of the election. Accompanied by nobles and other notable personages of their kingdoms, they gather in the temple of Huitzilopochtli to witness the consecration of the great chosen one and to see him receive the flint knife—which he will one day hand on to his successor, upon the same altar—as a symbol of the enormous power entrusted to him.

"The impressive procession leaves the house of Moctezuma and moves toward the great *teocalli* in the following order: the feudatory lords of the various states lead the march, each one carrying the insignia of his rank; they are followed by the nobles with their emblems of office and rank. Then come the kings of Acolhuacán and Tacuba, firm allies of Mexico. At the last walks the elected king, surrounded by splendid warriors. He greets the public as he moves forward, wearing only the *máxtlatl,* the loincloth; the robes and ornaments of the imperial office will be presented to him during the ceremony.

"Upon the steps of the *teocalli* the high priest awaits him, surrounded by religious functionaries who will assist him in the consecration. After the oath, the high priest stains a cloth with three colors and lays it across the king's chest; then he covers him with an *ichcahuipilli.* To the tricolored band he fastens a small vessel containing a mysterious powder, an amulet against spells and calamities.

"The time has come for the charge to the new sovereign. He is congratulated for his accession to power and enjoined to govern well and to administer justice righteously. The new monarch replies that he will ever attempt to respect religions, show paternal affection toward the poor and try to unify and aggrandize the country. He promises to fulfill the religious duty which dictates that he live only for the happiness of his people.

"Immediately afterward Moctezuma, followed by his retinue, descends to the lower atrium and sets off toward his palace. Along the way he is congratulated by the populace and the nobility, receiving the oath of fidelity from all his vassals and above all from the warriors, who present their respects, offering tributes and rich gifts. The impressive ceremony takes place in the room known as *tlacateco*. Later follow public celebrations, with human sacrifices.

"Ilhuicamina has been in office only a few months when powerful neighboring realms begin a war. He understands that for the present he must hold off the intervention of Tenochtitlán, and he waits impatiently for a strong and honorable motive to join the hostilities. Wisely, he feigns neutrality, and his prudence increases the audacity of the other nations. Then a dastardly act—the sinking of two *acálotls* of Mexica—obliges the Aztec king to throw off his peaceful posture: Tenochtitlán allies itself with the powerful lordships of the north against the warlords who are trying to destroy the empire's unity.

"Moctezuma triumphs in the bloody war. At the end of his reign, victorious, he receives widespread public acclaim for his success, based on the expansion of the army—all the young Aztecs have been obliged to enlist."

"THE FIRST MOCTEZUMA owed his efficacious government to a large degree to the young Axayácatl, who unified all the lords and chiefs in a system that maintained absolute integrity in public affairs. He sent skillful *tlacuilos*, or emissary scribes, to the most distant regions, and even the vanquished warriors, formerly so proud, adopted the elevating teachings of the Aztec culture.

"To establish order in the provinces, garrisons of tiger knights were stationed in the principal cities; the local *tecuhtlis* were obliged to come to Tenochtitlán during certain periods to render accounts and tributes and were required to leave a son or other relative hostage in the imperial capital.

"Moctezuma promoted the progress of arts and sciences as well as that of war and social welfare. He encouraged useful activities. The entire country reflected the happy aspect that abundance and glory impart to a people. Zealous for the proper administration of justice, he also adopted many of Netzahualcóyotl's wise laws for the Texcocans.

"Suddenly the tireless labors stopped. Moctezuma fell gravely ill; he saw that the end of his days was drawing near. Until the final moment of his life he sustained the desire to serve, trying to preserve to the last the unity of his nation. He called the principal personages of his kingdom to the site where he lay dying. When they were all united to listen to their king, Moctezuma requested that the four electors choose Prince Axayácatl to succeed him, enumerating the qualities his choice possessed that were vital to the governing of the empire. It was a nomination totally free of personal preference; he was moved only by a lofty concern for the country's well-being.

"Axayácatl had distinguished himself on the battlefield. In addition to his valor, indispensable in a ruler, he possessed all the virtues which accompany a noble spirit. The flint and the regal crown *copilli* were delivered to him at the shrine of Huitzilopochtli, as had been done with all those who preceded him on the Aztec throne. Moctezuma Ilhuicamina left with his people an indelible memory of the many benefits his reign had provided. . . ."

"Yes," interrupted Copilli. "Although I was but a child, I remember the sad moment of his funeral rites. I mourned the Great Lord as if he had been a close relative."

V
Axayácatl

"NO EMPEROR of Anáhuac had had the political preparation, and so much sympathy and support from the masses, that your father, our Lord Axayácatl, enjoyed. He was the first who was not a soldier—he would have to earn certain privileges; it was a postwar period and a time of great calamities and epidemics in the countryside.

"You who lived under his reign, O Copilli, you will have seen the magnanimity and benevolence with which he treated all Aztecs, even those who were to betray him. At the same time you observed, young lord, that our country never resented the demands of a pilot as creative and dynamic as Axayácatl. To him we owe our people's new conception of the art of government. Thanks to his efforts and promptings, it was possible to harvest the fruits of good seeds that other kings had sown. He encouraged the production of corn and beans so that there would never be want in the nation's granaries, although later others abandoned the project. And although the economic and social development of our warriors, farmers and *macehuales*—vassals—achieved a brilliance that only the ideal sun of a Quetzalcóatl could provide, your wise father never neglected the spiritual well-being of the Aztecs. He tried to expand schools and conservatories, promoting the arts of the scribes and artisans, *tlacuilos* and *amantécatls*, and providing extraordinary buildings and services for our great house of studies, the Calmecac—source of wonder to all nations, reminiscent of the proud Huehuetlapallán.

"Noble Copilli, you are the descendent of a man who made the Aztec throne a new world of unrealized potential. Axayácatl was the first of our monarchs to realize that he could not alone wage the great battle of government and defend Tenochtitlán against its enemies without provoking ill will within the country. Thus you will see that the just king appears in the hieroglyphics of the pyramid surrounded by noble warriors and legislators, brave *tlacatécatls* and *cihuacóatls* who acted as his ministers in the governing of the empire. You will note that they were as noble, intelligent and educated as he was and that many were his youthful companions in the classrooms of the Calmecac. He honored with his friendship those who were worthy of it and trusted them without reservation, for he knew that friendship is a gift more precious than the crown itself.

"There is agreement among those who have recounted the history of this popular emperor's Tenochtitlán in long codices and day-by-day engravings. They coincide in praising his personal qualities and remarking his daring as a leader who never abused his power nor used it to dominate the weak.

"The *tobeyos* of our land planted the prodigious seed of Father Centli—the maize that grows high and lush as if it wished to touch the sandals of Tonacatatecutli, and the indispensable bean. The *calpullis* which had lacked water began to enjoy its use thanks to dams planned by architects and built by slaves. And never have fields so full of corn, beans and gourds been seen as in your father's time.

"When the cycle was completed, the calendar marked the end of Axayácatl's power. He convened the electors of the *tlatocán* to advise them of his choice for a successor to govern Anáhuac. He did so in the same spirit that informed all his acts —the pure love for Tenochtitlán, land of his birth. The electors contemplated the needs of the following twenty-five years, aware that there must be continuity in the next *tlalpilli*. Many begged that he extend the cycle, ignore the calendar, and he responded, 'No. My father died defending the cycle; I too fought to maintain it.'

"And then he handed on the flint knife to his successor, who ended Axayácatl's life with a single blow. Tamoanchán was filled with his spirit."

THUS SPOKE MOXOTLI, the narrator, reading from the inscriptions on the great pyramid blessed by Tláloc. With the end of the narration, transcribed in miraculous hieroglyphs upon the huge stone, Copilli could not hold back tears of love and nostalgia.

And he ordered his chief *tlacuilo* to record the events of his own life, a story which later, in its turn, would also be inscribed in stony hieroglyphics.

VI
Childhood

Here Prince Copilli begins the dictation of his life story.

AS MY LORD TLÁLOC well knows, I did not have an easy childhood for all that I was the son of the great Axayácatl. I remember my father being unusually strict with me. He felt that I required a special kind of education, one that would make me worthy of my princely title and his noble lineage. He realized, as he so often reminded me, that what in any other child would be considered heroism would in my case be regarded as mere boldness; what in any other noble would be looked upon as culture, in me would be no more than instruction; and what in another would be deemed wit, in Prince Copilli would be severely condemned as an unseemly desire for calling attention to himself.

"Son," my king and lord used to say, "see everything, observe and do all, but only in your heart and mind, for in this court there are many who will flatter you while speaking ill of you behind your back, and the hand that caresses you today will not balk at stabbing you tomorrow. Prepare yourself, my little prince, prepare yourself so that you may know, judge and help all men. Study, be strong and persevere. Be cool of mind and passionate of heart . . . and remember this—whatever happens it is neither for you nor against you; it is simply life . . ."

How right he was, wise Axayácatl! More than once, weeping in a secluded corner of the palace, I remembered his advice and regretted not having acted on it. And so I think of my childhood as being twofold: I was both the son of a man and the son of a king.

When I was very small, before my father had ascended the throne, I came to live in Tenochtitlán. My father, if strict, was always kind and loving toward me. My mother, of course, sweetened my early years even more with her tenderness, especially since she knew that she would soon be separated from me.

"How hard it is to be the mother of a prince and the wife of a king," she said to me once, while we stood at the lakeside watching the gray herons wading in the water. "The duties of state and court snatch our little ones away from us, and the time we spend in their company, which is all we have, passes more fleetingly than the budding of a flower." At the time I did not comprehend my mother's tears. When I left her side to begin my studies at the Telpochcalli, I understood.

When I was born, the *Tonalpouhqui* predicted that I would be a valiant warrior with a bleeding heart. My parents always interpreted the omen to mean that I would go to war and that after winning many victories in the field of honor I would be slain by my enemies.

As the son of the Great Lord I was registered, twenty days after my birth, for the two colleges: the Calmecac and the Telpochcalli. I was to spend my childhood in the Telpochcalli. There I would receive my first lessons, which included religious instruction; in the Calmecac I would learn how to defend myself and conquer an enemy, and train to be a gallant captain of the Tenochcas. I would prepare myself so that later I might join whichever order of knights for which my merits destined me.

My father used to relate to me how the *teopixque*, or priest, who received him when he took me to him as a babe in arms, frowned when he beheld my trembling body, for he thought I would not live. This *teopixque*, known as Huécatl, was later my tutor and loved me dearly.

When I was old enough to run about I played with children of my own age, for the most part sons of nobles. However, I spent a great deal of time with the *taparrabientos chilpayates* of the *macehuales*, for in them—possibly more so than in the noble children—I found very good companions and faithful friends. On one occasion I inadvertently wounded two of my friends—one a noble, the other a plebeian—with the same arrow accidentally loosed from my bow. The patrician ran off crying to complain to his father about me, but the plebeian, through his pain, assured me he understood it had been an accident; it was he who consoled me. Perhaps at the time I did not appreciate his behavior as much as I do now in memory.

When I was ten I was admitted into the Telpochcalli, or sacerdotal school, directed by the great Telpuchtlato. There, for the first time, I learned what rigid discipline was. We had to get up with the first rays of the sun, make sacrifices and suffer privations. Rich and poor students alike were punished with unremitting severity. Most of my companions were not there to train for the priesthood but simply to study the elementary sciences before becoming *pochtecas*, merchants, or officials in the administration of Tenochtitlán, or until they were old enough to marry. Others, like myself, after completing our lower education—which included basic concepts of military art—would go on to specialize in the science of war within the walls of the exclusive Calmecac.

There were some very interesting boys in the Telpochcalli. I only vaguely recall their names, but their actions are engraved on my memory. I remember one particular occasion when a companion and myself were severely punished for a misdemeanor: instead of painting our bodies black and leaving our faces unpainted, according to the rule of the house, we did the very opposite, turning up for roll call with coal-black faces and our bodies completely clean. For penance we had to sweep the Telpochcalli for a whole moon, get up before everybody else for midnight worship and light the fire at the crack of dawn.

I think that of all the lessons we were taught at the sacerdotal school, the one which I learned with greatest fervor and which has stood me in greatest stead in my life was to have faith and trust in Tláloc. It was under his auspices that my mother placed me, for, as I was later told, I came into the world in the midst of a torrential rainstorm. I used to prepare the altar of the Lord of the Rain with a special sense of joy; when we had to pierce ourselves with the sacrificial maguey thorns, rather than dedicate my pain to Huitzilopochtli, I would ask for it to be offered up with the *copalli* to the Tlalocán.

As far as the rest of my studies went, on the whole I acquitted myself well in all of them. I was particularly drawn to the art of hieroglyphics, which I quickly mastered, as I did the sweet songs of King Netzahualcóyotl, of whom my father spoke so frequently, relating how he had joined forces with the great Mexica king Ixcóatl to form the most powerful alliance of Anáhuac.

Once, during the rainy season, my favorite period and

which I found singularly agreeable, all us *yaoyizques* of the Telpochcalli were taken to Texcoco to attend a feast known in that region as the *etzacualiztli*. The celebrations were being held in honor of the goddess Chalchiutlicue. We made the journey on foot under the close vigil of Huécatl, at that time a *tiachcauh* or prefect of the academy. On the way, I argued against this Alcolhua feast, maintaining that such honors should be reserved for Tláloc. I remember going so far as to say—to the taunts of my companions—that I would do my best to spoil the festivities. I do not know if Tláloc took my side, but with the help of some strange force I had never experienced before, I managed it.

The *etzacualiztli* festivities always began with the making of signs and the offering up of cornstalks and bean bushes to the goddess in thanks for the abundant harvest made possible by the rains; then the Texcocans would sacrifice a young maiden in the waters of their lake. I was watching the opening ceremonies in the company of some other *yaoyizques* when my attention was drawn to several highly ornate litters, half covered by curtains of liana blossoms, *xochimécatl,* and bearing Alcolhua priests escorting a young girl dressed in blue, with black hair flowing down her back. As we had been given preferential places, I happened to be standing very close to the litters and had no difficulty following the conversation. Moments later she would be decapitated in honor of Chalchiutlicue. My indignation knew no bounds at the sight of the maid crying bitterly, aware of the horrible fate that awaited her, as the priests tried in vain to convince her that she was the envy of all the other maidens in Texcoco. Moved partly by compassion, partly by my desire to break up the festivities, I slipped away from the other *yaoyizques* and through the rows of unsuspecting spectators, approaching the litters from behind. Tlallanxóchitl—Subterranean Flower—as the child was called, seemed to have stopped weeping; two last tears rolled down her dusky cheeks. Entranced and silent, I stood watching, until one of the priests noticed me. His face impassive, he harshly ordered me to return to my place. I did not obey.

Instead, taking advantage of the fact that the litters had been laid on the ground, I leaped forward, seized Tlallanxóchitl, practically tearing her from the arms of the priest, and took to flight. Immediately pandemonium spread. The confusion protected us. The girl, a sweet and gentle burden, was terrified and said nothing. I kept on running.

I took cover behind some trees, then doubled back, throwing my pursuers off the track. In a few moments we came upon a shack, and without hesitating I dashed into it with the maiden. Inside, to my surprise, was a group of women, and more surprisingly, one of them held out her arms to Tlallanxóchitl and, tenderly gathering her to her breast, called her "my little girl."

"That is her mother," a *tícitl*, or sorceress, standing among them told me. "Chalchiutlicue herself has performed the miracle of her salvation."

I was not exactly pleased by this arbitrary overlooking of my clever intervention, but for the moment I was happy to find myself safe.

"Hurry!" the sorceress cried anxiously. "Let us go into the cave behind the house. When they come they will find here only Zolín, the child's mother, and they will go back . . . no time to lose!" Quick to act on the old medicine woman's advice, we took refuge in the cave, which was dark and very damp because of a river flowing through it to the lake. The cave entrance was almost invisible to anyone unfamiliar with the area. Zolín had remained behind in her modest home.

We remained in the cave a long time, not emerging until the *tícitl* considered it safe under the cover of the night shadows. Tlallanxóchitl and I came out hand in hand. Our fingers had met and intertwined in the darkness. My fourteen years were telling me something about the small frail girl, something I could not explain: I squeezed her hand. Outside all was calm, although at the lake and in the sugar-cane fields and on the mountainside we could see the torches of our pursuers. I certainly spoiled the celebration, I thought to myself with satisfaction.

Zolín came out of the shack and joined us. The sorceress, an extremely cunning woman, ordered her to don a man's *áyatl* and stick war feathers in her hair and dress her daughter the same way. The good woman was quick to comply; shortly she and Tlallanxóchitl came out of the house disguised as young men.

"Now, take a torch," instructed the sorceress, "and leave by the main path to Cholula. The journey is very long. Once you have left the region of the lake you will be out of danger, for nobody will know you. If you meet with any warriors call out loudly, 'Have you found them yet?' Then continue on your way without hiding; try to look as though you were searching for the fugitives in the bushes. The darkness and Chalchiutlicue will protect you."

Tlallanxóchitl turned to me. "We have a house in Cholula," she said. "Come and visit me there. I shall never forget how you rescued me . . . I love you." And on uttering these strange last words, she left with her mother.

Rooted to the spot, I watched the bright flame of the torch fade into the darkness. The words of the *tícitl* startled me out of my trance.

"And now what are we going to do with you, *yaoyizque?* I don't even know your name."

"As for the first point, do not worry; I can look after myself. As for the second, that is simple; I am Copilli, the son of Axayácatl." And saying this, I was suddenly remorseful over having abandoned the ranks of my young companions, and I departed, leaving the sorceress stunned.

Huécatl and my friends received me with expressions of concern.

"Wherever have you been, Copilli? We thought the men with the panther faces had got you."

"What men?" I asked.

"The ones that carried off the maiden. Don't you know? There was a great uproar because thirty men or devils with panther faces attacked the Alcolhua priests and ran away with the sacrificial virgin. Where were you?"

"I was bored by the festivities so I went off to the mountain of Tláloc," I replied. As we made our way home I did not know whether to laugh, to think about Tlallanxóchitl, to meditate—or indeed to consider myself a worthy instrument of the lord of Tlalocán, chosen to illustrate his celestial power.

I relate this incident not because I wish to celebrate my courage or daring—neither of which virtues applied here since I merely acted in response to blind impulse when I impetuously rushed to Tlallanxóchitl's rescue—but rather because it had special consequences for me. First, it made me abhor human sacrifice; second, it taught me to know love; finally, it burdened me with a secret that I could not divulge to anyone for some time, for fear that my beloved maiden would be discovered and slain together with her mother.

While lying on my bed of matting in the Telpochcalli some nights after the strange events, I kept thinking of how the girl had looked at me. The more I tossed and turned on my *petate* the more distinctly I heard that phrase "I love you," so childlike and yet so painfully haunting. "Subterranean Flower," I thought—subterranean like the water in the cave where our hands had touched, under the murmuring sign of a river created by Tláloc. . . .

But after a few months I was free of the obsession, which faded into merely an enchanting memory. We *yaoyizques* were now sufficiently prepared to leave the Telpochcalli: now we must choose a station in life in accordance with our vocations, the duties of lineage or the desires of our families—particularly these last two considerations, because one shapes his life in terms of what he wants to be.

My own destiny involved entering the Calmecac within the next moon. When I took my leave of Huécatl and my companions, they presented me with a rose-colored shell pendant on a jade necklace, in token of our friendship. Never shall I forget the moment when I left the academy to return to the *tecpan,* or palace. The first surprise awaited me at the door of the Telpochcalli itself: three warriors and several *macehuales* bearing a marvelous litter adorned with pheasant and peacock feathers. Their faces were familiar to me, although I did not recall their names.

An eagle knight addressed me. "*Quáchic*—Prince—our lord Axayácatl sends greeting and awaits you at the lake with our empress, in the very spot where you played as a child. We will take you there, illustrious Copilli."

Now I am a man, I reflected as I seated myself on the litter.

VII

The Calmecac

ALTHOUGH I FELT quite the young man, a *yaoyizque* soon to enter the Calmecac, I was unable to sustain the piercing gaze of my father; his eyes seemed to bore into my very soul.

I knew that to him I had been no more than a rebellious and willful youth with a normal childhood. Among my Telpochcalli companions I had been neither the most distinguished nor the dullest. Now, however, he seemed to view me in a different light. He automatically granted me more distinction and authority within the palace; at the same time he was firmer with me and indulged me less. Henceforth I was Prince Copilli, and soon I would be old enough to receive the title of *tecuhtli*, go to war and sit in the Tlatocán, if I so wished.

I realized that my father had faith in me and I was filled with pride. My father and lord was confident that one day, with the protecting influence of Tláloc, I would be given command. And since authority always brings responsibility, he took pains to ensure that I received special instruction in the arts and sciences, especially in the honorable virtues of good government, in which all rulers should be well versed.

I learned more from his advice than from all the lessons I would receive in the Calmecac. I remember how one day we strolled together near the springs of Chapultépetl; then we sat in the shade of a leafy tree and he told me the marvelous story of Quetzalcóatl. I had heard the story on numerous occasions, but coming from him, so wise, so just and kind, it acquired new life and a hitherto unknown charm.

"Everyone believes, my son, that the figure of Quetzalcóatl is simply a myth or legend sustained by the priestly caste, but I must tell you that his existence was real, physical, patent. Quetzalcóatl is not merely a representation, but also a man. And his conch shell sounds not with the hollow echo of fantasy but with the sharp pitch of reality.

"I myself did not know Quetzalcóatl, but my father and my father's father tell how they heard from their forefathers the traditional story of his existence. From generation to generation, we have passed down the wise advice which he left us on the governing of the people, for he was blessed by a rare and enriching experience.

"That is why, my son, in the meetings you have had occasion to attend, you will have heard the nobles and lords address me as Quetzalcóatl. We who hold the reins of government in Anáhuac are all Quetzalcóatl, for we follow and apply his teachings.

"I must instruct you in some of his most important precepts and I hope you will never forget them, wherever you may be.

"Politics, or the art of public government, very often is more important than war.

"You can only govern men by serving them. When you see that your orders will not be obeyed, do not impose them, but seek a new path; otherwise authority is lost. Remember, my son, that he who governs haphazardly will find himself at the mercy of the unexpected. The rule should be: consider, examine and weigh well all issues, no matter how small, and then act quickly and decisively. That is why public government is never an easy matter.

"Do not surround yourself with friends who are too enterprising, for they will take it on themselves to give their own orders and misinterpret yours. When many rule, few obey, Copilli.

"Remember it is easier to decree laws than to apply them, and that the laws you have received from your predecessors are not sacred; respect their good qualities but rectify their shortcomings.

"When one becomes king, Copilli, one truly begins to understand the problems of the nation, although it is impossible to resolve them all. If only the dead kings could, from the Tamoanchán, counsel the new ones! But the latter have the memory of the former's reigns for guidance in the problems and needs of government, and their power is enhanced by that of the deceased monarchs. And because his labors, thoughts and deeds are so arduous and complex, the governing *tecuhtli,* upon whom all final decisions rest, must be strong and well prepared."

As my father spoke these words, I remained silent as a stone, studying the countenance of great Axayácatl.

"Always be good to your fellow men," the king continued. "Choose your friends wisely and cherish them until death. Learn to forgive all wrongs save treason, for men are human and we are all equal, but treachery is the offense that distinguishes one man from another. Remember that you have not attained your position by your own endeavors and therefore should not be overproud of it."

"But I am proud of you, father," I said sincerely.

"Keep your proper place, which is far more difficult," he replied, "and then I too will be proud of you."

"Why do you tell me all these things, lord, if I am not to succeed you to the throne?"

"One can never receive too much counsel, Copilli, and this that I have given you on the art of government will also serve in ruling your life. May the gods always protect you and keep you mindful of it."

Then we took the path of the *ahuehuetes* back to the royal litters, which bore us to the palace. On the way we passed through the principal avenues, which were lined with people who had come to venerate my father and express their affection.

I WAS NOW READY to enter the Calmecac, which was situated opposite our palace and adjoined the great Teocalli. There I would live for several moons, learning the principal sciences, the laws of my country and the difficult arts of prudence and humility. On my arrival in the company of other *yaoyizques* from the Telpochcalli, I had to submit to the initiation ceremony. This was extremely painful and humiliating, but necessary in order to curb the pride of those who would hold in their hands the destiny of their fellow men and hence must needs dominate their passions. During the ceremony we neophyte *yaoyizques* danced completely naked in the patio before the great *cihuacóatl* of Tenochtitlán, the director of the Calmecac, and the other young men, most of whom were adorned with the insignia of the *cuauhtli, océlotl* or *miztli* knights.

The dance went on until the hour in which the sun reached the top of the Teocalli. Then the *cuauhtli* and *océlotl* knights— not the *miztli,* who were of higher rank and could not demean themselves—shaved our heads and daubed our bodies with black paint like that which we had used in the Telpochcalli. We did penance until nightfall, when we retired to our beds, our eyes brimming with tears, but not uttering a murmur of protest.

IN THE MORNINGS at the Calmecac we performed martial exercises, among others training in the handling of the *cuauhololli,* or mace, the battle-ax and the shield or *chimalli.* Utilizing weapon rests, known as *átlatl,* which we had never used before, we learned to throw *tlocohtli,* or darts, with speed and precision. These sessions were called *yaomachtl.* We always looked forward to them eagerly. Our main desire was eventually to be admitted to an order of the knights, like the older students or the soldiers who made up the permanent guard of the Calmecac. Later we had marching drills in the patio and practiced campaign maneuvers outside the building—once going as far as Texcoco and back the same day.

At sunset we studied the art of the *tlacuilos,* as well as astronomy, arithmetic, languages of neighboring peoples and oratory and drama in order to learn how to express ourselves better. At midnight we prayed, and then the priests and warriors in charge of our training saw to it that their disciples went to bed. They even kept watch on the Calmecac walls to prevent anyone's trying to climb over them. This breach of discipline was punishable by death and brought dishonor to the culprit's family.

I submitted to the routine and the exercises with the full conviction that it was for my good. I was spurred on by my ambition and my desire to help my people in whatever way I could. I had gone through the initiation ceremonies like all the other *yaoyizques;* the only difference from most of my companions was my zeal to learn more in less time, so that I could rapidly forge for myself rank and position.

The day came when we had to leave for a campaign in what were called the Flowery Wars. They formed us in squadrons of five, under a *tequihua;* followed by an *otómitl* and five other bowmen. They placed us as the rearguard of the regular army's mighty legion, under the leadership of a *tlacatécatl* whose name I no longer recall, although he distinguished himself through his skill and strategic ability. Each *yaoyizque* was provided with an *ichcahuipilli,* a battle tunic of strong cotton, and a plumeless helmet. We carried *itácatls* or rucksacks containing our provisions, and darts, *chimallis* and maces.

Before our departure we offered sacrifices to Ypana-Huitzilopochtli. We prayed for strength to kill the enemy. My heart was beating so violently that I felt as if my breast would burst. I could not contain myself, so much did I look forward to taking prisoners so that I might rise in the ranks and win my father's approval. None of us knew the route of our column. I speculated that we would march to the lands of the Huejotzingas or Atlixqueños, ancient rivals of our people, attack their border garrisons and take prisoners for sacrifice in the Coatlán, the temple my father and lord had constructed; or that, going in another direction, we would lay siege to the indefatigable Chalcans and engage them in another traditional skirmish. However, after several hard days' marches when we had crossed the central valleys and the sierra, I realized my mistake. Being a mere *yaoyizque,* I could not address the *tlacatécatl* directly but had to go through my *tiachcauh,* who led me to our general.

"Great *tecuhtli,*" I said, "could you tell me the destination of our journey? I see the nights pass through the sky and still we have not engaged in combat. Are we simply going on a long march?"

"Prince Copilli," he replied, "know that our king and lord Axayácatl has ordered me to put you and your companions to the same great test of obtaining prisoners for sacrifice that he himself underwent before he was crowned. Only thus will he know if you are a worthy descendant of his blood and stock. You all must be valiant and loyal so that you may receive the communion of his flesh and blood."

"You mean, then, that we are going to Huauxyaca, great *tecuhtli?*"

"Farther, Prince—to the great Tehuantépetl, that valiant and savage city your father, our just king, devastated with blood and fire many moons ago and which has now risen again proud and mighty."

The Tehuantepecas! We, a mere handful of *yaoyizques* and imperial officers, were to snatch from this indomitable race slaves for sacrifice to Ypana-Huitzilopochtli! I think I trembled. But my callow body bore the badge of the Aztec youth—the insignia of the Calmecac!—the symbols of valor and daring, boldness and obedience. My father knew well the peril against which we would be measured: it was his judicious orders that sent us into it. By my honor as a prince, let his belief in me not be disappointed! I felt courageous and loyal.

We traversed many countries green as jade, abounding with animals that I had never before seen, and which we hunted for food during the journey. Mist rose from the earth as if to repel the invasion of our valiant troops. The sun scorched our exhausted bodies and bathed us in sweat. Our feet felt like burning coals. We were approaching the enemy.

Once we had penetrated into the heart of Mixtec country we marched only by night. Thus we avoided dangerous confrontations and exhaustion from the heat. Two *yaoyizques* had perished of the fever, a very common sickness in those regions, as our wise priest Mazatlayauhqui told us; he explained that the cold blood of Coatlicue's serpents took possession of the unfortunate victims, who then died. We soon became accustomed to sleeping by day and advancing stealthily in the shadows of the night, like coyotes and *cacomixtles*—and like the just Alcolhua king Netzahualcóyotl, who wandered in the valleys and mountains before reconquering his domains.

Then finally one night we halted in the middle of the jungle. Our *tlacatécatl* decided we should make camp until the next full moon in order to give us time to regain our strength and sharpen our flint knives; meanwhile, several scouts were sent to Tehuantépetl to determine our distance from the city. It happened that we were close by. We had been careful to follow a meandering route in order to confuse any possible spies, although it was unlikely that there were any because of the conflict between the Mixtec and Zapotec dominions over the Tehuantepec hegemony. Their quarrel had arisen over the limits of their borders, which they had not been able to settle to their mutual satisfaction. One night the scouts returned with good news: the Tehuantepecas were feasting; they were celebrating the birth of Petela, the king's firstborn, who had been named after a divinity. They had given themselves up to an orgy of excess, drinking strange fermented brews known only in those lands, in which were embodied wicked spirits, worse even than those of the *neutle*. They were offering up their frenzied revelries to the continuity of the dynasty. This was the propitious moment to surprise them and take the few city guards as prisoners.

The combat would have far greater meaning for me than for any other *yaoyizque*. It would test my spirit and mettle against that of my father and lord. This would be the opportunity either to rise to a place among the military nobility or to be debased by the contempt of my superiors. We waited impatiently for the sheltering night shadows, under which we would attack the Tehuantepecas. That day it seemed to me the sun would never set.

At dusk our chief ordered us to advance to a narrow pass. This was formed not by the flanks of mountains but by huge tropical trees whose dense foliage made it impossible for large contingents to penetrate.

The *cuauhtli* and *océlotl* warriors ordered us to dig a great pit many paces long, deep enough to hold one man standing on the shoulders of another. Working hurriedly, by midnight we had dug an enormous pit in the center of the narrow pathway; in the bottom we fixed upright large sharpened branches that would impale the body of a man. Finally we covered the surface with light branches and dead leaves. Our *tlacatécatl*'s strategy was to lure the enemy to the trap and kill them in the confusion that would ensue as the first warriors tumbled into the pit. He distributed some *yaoyizques*, under the command of our *tequihua*, among the trees lining the path; these were *otómitl*, or archers, well provided with arrows.

The rest of us, under the leadership of our *tlacatécatl*, skirted the pit and continued along the narrow path toward Tehuantépetl. We reached the outer walls of the town in the early hours of the morning. The city had abandoned itself to orgy. We did not even meet the customary night patrol which all towns maintain to keep the public peace. The first streets we came to were deserted. Shoulder to shoulder we advanced, carrying in our left hands the *chimalli* and in our right the *tepuztocalli* or spear, making no sound. Suddenly a half-naked man emerged from a house, completely drunk. Seeing us, he began to applaud, thinking it was a military parade in honor of Petela. A *cuauhtli*'s mace convinced him, too late, that we were no friendly troop. The wounded man screamed in terror. In the nearby shacks dogs began to bark. Our chief gave the order to spread out; the battle charge from the golden *huéhuetl* echoed throughout the city.

Our squadrons split up: while some attacked from the south side of the central temple, we swung around and entered from the north, shouting, howling and loosing arrows. Our troops surrounded the square and burst in from one side of the temple. Some Tehuántepec soldiers were armed, but even so the carnage was terrible. My arm was driven by the insupportable heat I had suffered, by the fears of the last few dark nights, the exhaustion of the long marches and the desire to see myself elevated to a high rank. My *yaoyizque* companions must have felt the same: their maces ceaselessly crushed skulls and their knives drove into breasts with that frightful sound that not even the prolonged boom of our victorious *huéhuetl* could drown.

We closed in on a group of warriors who had managed to regroup in the turmoil and were resolutely defending their arms. Shortly we drove them back with many losses through the dwellings toward the city gates. They retreated in confusion toward the narrow pass, looking back to check our advance. We were content to cut them off, and left our *otómitls* hidden among the trees, in case we were pursued. Despite the clarity of the night our *tlacatécatl* did not want to run the risk of our becoming confused and attacking our own men.

It was dawn. The city was all but deserted. A few women and children wandered tearfully through the streets, offering us valuables if we would go away and leave them in peace. The king and his wife, together with their infant Petela, had managed to escape under the protection of the palace guard. As frequently happens on such occasions, they had not attended the feast held in their honor. Among the warriors trapped in the square and those who lay down their weapons before the attack of our bowmen, we had taken as many prisoners as the fingers of thirty hands.

After killing our mortally wounded—we could not take them with us without putting our own lives in danger—we formed our column and hastily abandoned the city. By now news of the sacking had spread to the neighboring towns, carried by the king himself and the other survivors. The columns of smoke rising from the crops provided further evidence of our victory. Our chief had ordered the fields burned to demonstrate that our punishment was not only present death but future famine. And thus we devastated the rebellious town which had always resisted the dominion of our kings, natural lords of the Anáhuac. Around our necks hung chains of gold and emerald, obsidian black as night, and singular figures perfectly carved. Animal skins, robes, mother-of-pearl *malácatls,* turtle shells and weapons of flint and rare woods completed our booty. Finally we had raided the houses, particularly those of the *pochtecas,* merchants, for food in plenty for our troops and prisoners: the return journey would be far more arduous than the outgoing one.

We knew we might be harassed by princes of domains friendly toward Tehuantépetl. Emboldened by our victory, we felt that no obstacle was too great for us—with only a handful of our men we would have attacked the most powerful of foes. But as we were worn out by our exertions and heavily laden, the first day's march could have been fatal for us. Our *tlacaté-*

catl therefore wisely led us via the coast rather than taking us straight north, thereby throwing the Tehuantepecas off.

Weary and perspiring, our backs scorched by the early afternoon sun, we came to a coastal region where the Tehuantepecas kept their *acálotls* and ships. After a brief combat with the somnolent garrison, we took over their canoes. We rowed day and night over a tranquil sea, in sight of the coast. Satisfied finally that we had left our enemies behind, we made camp on the shore. We were exhausted and our hands were bleeding, but we were joyful, for we had become men, to the glory of Tenochtitlán. That evening we celebrated our triumph with *yaomachtl,* martial exercises reliving the violent scenes our novice hearts had just experienced. A count was made of the prisoners taken by each *yaoyizque:* the rank conferred on each young man would depend on the number of captives he had taken.

Several of us *yaoyizques* had taken more than five prisoners and had thereby earned the right to join the order of the *miztlitecuhtli* or lion knights, the highest military rank of the nobility. Our companions and the *tlacatécatl* himself congratulated us. Henceforth we were entitled to use the *ichcahuipilli,* as yet without colors, for we would receive military status in a special ceremony on our return to Tenochtitlán.

When the festivities had concluded and a guard had been mounted over the prisoners, I lay down on the beach to sleep. The heat was stifling. The sea breeze helped, but I was unable to sleep. At first my thoughts whirled like a flock of birds of ill omen. Then certain images began to stand out. I saw the horror of the slaughter, the screaming, the fire, the confusion. I saw again the point of my spear sinking into the golden flesh of the Tehuantepeca.

And the blood, above all the blood! There before my eyes it oozed stickily between my fingers, a ghostly red. And then a great bellow of laughter: Huitzilopochtli, his cadaverous arms strangling Tláloc, my protector, noble and fecund god. I had killed; I had killed without reason. *Does war truly make men of us?* I asked myself. *Can we justify killing the enemy with impunity, just because he is the enemy? Does mere victory give us the right to steal?* The sound of the sea dashing against the rocks evoked the sound of the *técpatl* crushing the breasts of the enemy, and the sound accused me, Prince Copilli, proud son of the lord Axayácatl, of having committed a deed for which I had prepared myself with religious fervor.

"Tláloc," I cried out in desperation, "come to my aid! Save me!" Like a hunter's bubbling cauldron of meat, my thoughts boiled with the awful knowledge that I was a murderer; worse than this, the realization that the power of the kingdom—which tomorrow might be mine—depended on the *tzompantli* with its thousands of skulls. Then I asked myself, *What would become of us if we did not kill? Would our foes respect us?*

Overwhelmed by these thoughts, I brooded for a time, until a gentle rain brought peace. The secret voice of my protector, great Tláloc, spoke within me. "Now that you have killed and suffered for having done so, your heart is no longer like the timid deer, but rather the indomitable puma: gall and obsidian. Now you are ready to know and confront your like. In your world rule does not have to mean force, though there will be times when you must use it. Wise Netzahualpilli curbed the defiance of some of his subjects with prudent laws inspired by the decrees of his father: *that* is the path, Prince Copilli. Though it may seem strange to you, by staining your hands with blood you have acquired purity of spirit. Now, conserve it!

"There still remains the ceremony before Huitzilopochtli. The hearts of the prisoners will be offered up and you will eat of their flesh in a glorious communion with those valiant men and the god of war."

After a time the somber rhythm of the waves gave way to the gentle beating of the *teponaxtlis.* The fever passed. I slept, caressed by the night breeze.

VIII
Anointment

WHAT A MARVELOUS CITY is ours. The more we travel and know other cities and lands, the bigger and more prosperous it seems. After the long journey to Tehuantépetl and the exhausting marches from the place known as Acapulco, Tenochtitlán rose before my eyes, a proud and noble city. That is how I remember seeing her when my companions and

I returned home from the Flowery War. I was now ready to become a *tecuhtli.*

We entered the city from the land of Tlalpán, after crossing the valleys of Cuauhnáuac and the mountains. We sent messengers ahead to announce our arrival. Jubilant multitudes headed by priests and warriors came to give a heroes' welcome to a Calmecac army which included among its ranks a son of the emperor.

The avenues and waterways were filled with splendid litters and brightly colored canoes bearing persons of every class and occupation. Crowds of people, some sincerely joyous, others merely curious, swarmed into the place called Tzollinco—place of quails—in order to welcome us. Nobles and plebeians alike awaited us.

When our group came into sight, the high priest in charge of the reception ordered the sacrifice of ten Chalcan virgins, who had been fattened for just such a solemn occasion; we were to be given a cup of their blood as soon as we arrived: this ancient custom brings honor to a town and fortifies the warriors. When we had tasted the fruits of the offering, our *yaoyizque* companions who had not accompanied us, together with the students of the Telpochcalli and the priests of the Great Temple, performed religious dances commemorating the pilgrimage of our people, their first settlement in the lake, and the victories of recent epochs, achieved with the aid of Quetzalcóatl.

The people were jubilant. They bore colorful plumes and obsidian, paintings of the most varied hues and diverse origins, gold and silver ornaments, capes of cotton and *ichcahuipillis* decorated with *quetzal* plumes; in the background the *huéhuetls* and *teponaxtlis* echoed joyful songs. A great lord— I do not remember his name—bore the effusive greetings of my father, the emperor, to our *tlacatécatl.* He said that my father was pleased to have entrusted the education of his son Copilli to so illustrious a man and skillful a general. Then, addressing me through the *quachic,* he said, "I congratulate you, young Prince, for by your deeds you have proved yourself worthy of your father, our great lord Axayácatl!" I could hardly contain my emotion at feeling that I had won the esteem of the wise emperor.

The festivities continued. The mingled sounds of music, sacerdotal hymns and the beat of the dance rose and filled the air; I too danced and sang so that my ecstatic prayer of gratitude and fulfillment would reach Tláloc.

AT THAT TIME I had several dear and faithful friends. With their help I embarked on all sorts of adventures. My oldest friends I had first met when I was a student in the Telpochcalli. We were a close-knit group, as ready for play or rest as for the arduous tasks requiring study, application and the aid of the gods. From many moons ago up to this very moment when I set down my life story for this pyramid, they have always been at my side when I needed them and have never betrayed me. Our friendship has developed into a surpassing bond, and we are inseparable. In this union of trust I have but followed the advice and example of my father, lord Axayácatl. It was he who taught me that the spiritual riches of friendship are our most treasured possession. Several of these friends were fellow disciples from the Calmecac and had fought in the Flowery Wars. Others I met during that experience, when I earned the right to be anointed *tecuhtli*.

When one has earned an honor, the moments preceding its recognition are the longest of all. It was so in my case. I had arrived triumphant from the Tehuantepec region, after taking prisoners and killing a number of enemies. I had passed the supreme test. Now it only remained for me to be awarded the title of *tecuhtli* and tiger knight in the ceremony of the *tecuhtlitonalpouhqui*. The high priest himself would anoint me.

Those who knew me well and whose friendship was not qualified by the fact that I was the son of the emperor congratulated me warmly on the approaching ceremony; others, however, spread rumors about me. They said that in the Calmecac I had received preferential treatment in the tests and that I had won the approval of my teachers not by my studies and personal gifts but as a result of direct influence of the Palace. According to them, I had been given special tests instead of the usual ones.

What hurt most was the fact that some of my detractors were fellow students. They never let an opportunity slip by to publicly malign me: they said that Prince Copilli's anointment and title of *tecuhtli* were a gift to raise him in the ranks of the nobility, not an honor that he had earned by his own efforts and talents. Their ill will increased to the extent of speaking disrespectfully of the Calmecac, that ancient school of learning that enjoyed well-deserved prestige among our people. Although I knew my detractors well, I did nothing to silence them.

I tried to complete the last of the five years, or *tlalpillis,* in less than the normal time. My request to take a special examination was denied me. I contended that attendance at the Calmecac should not be a privilege but instead a service providing the people greater opportunities to enjoy a splendid education and high culture.

Everything comes to those who wait—at last the day of my consecration came around with its accompanying hubbub. The Great Temple had not been specially adorned, for it was my request that it look as it did on any other day: any show of ostentation would have given my enemies further cause to criticize. My father and his ministers attended the ceremony. The latter honored me by carrying robes, *chimallis pantlis,* gold and obsidian, censers of jade and tiger skins, thus symbolizing their joy at my anointment and their approval of my deeds. Also present were the young and wise warriors, chiefs and guides of my class.

Then a vision of my past life flashed before me: my childhood and early youth, the black eyes of Tlallanxóchitl, the maiden I had rescued from the wrath of the Alcolhuas. That vision told me that Tláloc had not abandoned me, and that the special protective gods had always been with me. I knew that I, for my part, had always exerted myself as much as any other *yaoyizque* of my age, trying to mold my character as a warrior and earn the title of *tecuhtli*. This title, like that of my father, must distinguish me forever from those who had not had the fortune to fight for Tláloc for so many years, inside and outside the Calmecac, and receive this well-earned recognition.

That afternoon, as the sun was setting, hundreds of torches lit the center of Tenochtitlán. The column escorting me to the *teocalli* advanced with slow, solemn steps. The procession, accompanied by the hollow beat of the *teponaxtlis*, seemed to wrest tranquillity from the valley and shatter it into shards of somber colors. Trembling, wearing only a white *máxtlatl*, I walked behind great Axayácatl, who from his golden litter observed the tenscore slaves leading the procession. They were carrying the indispensable tribute for the ceremony in the *teocalli:* mantles and furs, exquisite ceramics and glittering jewels; one hundred *quetzals* in their cages—all evidence of my lord and father's generosity, and his pleasure that when he buried my umbilical cord in a battlefield to symbolize my destiny, it had not been in vain. Surrounded by priests and knights of the *océlotl, cuauhtli* and *mitztli* orders, I marched slowly behind the royal litter, my head bowed in humility. I lamented the fact that my critics prevented me from fully appreciating the solemnity of those moments.

The *tonalpouhqui* had indicated that the time was propitious. The cortege slowly ascended the steps of the Great Temple. When I reached the summit, I took from a cup the sharp maguey thorns prepared for the ceremony: with my blood I made the sacrifice to Tláloc and Huitzilopochtli. My submission and respect for the gods were imprinted on my flesh. I was aware of the stench of the *teotecuhtli* at my side; he was smeared with old blood. Taking an eagle's claw and a tiger bone thin as a needle, he pierced my nostrils and then hung two small emeralds from them. He explained to me that the eagle's claw would render me swift and implacable in war, while the bone of the *océlotl* would make me strong so that I might conquer my foes.

ANOINTMENT   73

My patience—a necessary virtue in men of high rank—was then to be put to the test. Several priests shouted insults at me, threw stones and pulled my hair. They tore my *máxtlatl* to shreds. Since I accepted these vexations without protest or defense, my serene conduct was approved with a prayer to the god of war. Later, as I had done the fasting and penances of the *tlamacazcalco* for many years, I proceeded to cense Huitzilopochtli with *copal* smoke which the priests prepared in a jade censer. Then they stripped away my *máxtlatl,* tied my hair with a red ribbon and adorned me with the *tlalpiloni* or war crest. I was dressed in the *ichcahuipilli, áyatl* and *máxtlatl,* which were embroidered as befitted my new status. The weapons of my new office were presented to me: the mace, the shield, the *átlatl* and the obsidian *técpatl.* Finally they placed in my hands the rich hide of an *océlotl,* whose head, with its open jaws, would serve as my helmet, insignia and protection. With the touch of the tiger skin, it came to me that in spite of my warrior blood there was something in me far superior to the animal strength bestowed upon me. In that moment I understood that the teachings of art and science meant more to me than those of war.

I was roused from my thoughts by the shouts of the priests and my relatives and the exclamations from the crowds of *macehuales* surrounding the *teocalli,* who up to then had remained in respectful silence. Shouts filled the air—not all of them exactly congratulatory. I realized that my enemies as well had come to the ceremony, simply to mock me now that I had received the coveted title of *tecuhtli.* My father turned his fine head, crowned with plumes, to the people with a gaze that was serene and profound, silent and eloquent. The murmuring subsided and finally ceased.

My lord Axayácatl took me by the hand and, addressing me as his favorite son, exclaimed, "You can best honor your rank and dignity by ignoring the iniquity of your detractors. Son, now you are a man and a prince; know that your position is close to the stars."

That was sufficient for me. I regained my composure and self-confidence. Smiling, I descended the steps of the *teocalli* to the cheers of those who were genuinely pleased to see me wearing the insignia of *tecuhtli*.

IX

The Legend
of Xochiquétzal

ONE AFTERNOON Tonacatecuhtli and his wife Tonacacihu-
atl, lords of the Heaven and the Earth, were getting ready to
send the young god Xochipilli, prince of the flowers, and his
sister Xochiquétzal, goddess of love, down to the world in the
form of mortals. The minor gods had to pass a test by fire:
they must descend to the earth as mortals and live there long

enough to show Tonacatecuhtli that they were worthy of their celestial status. If not, they would be thrown out of the Tamoanchán.

Xochipilli was jubilant. He knew that he was strong and agile, that no snare on earth could trap him like a coyote that wanders among the huts and devours rabbits. He knew he would return honored and triumphant to Tamoanchán, crowned with wreaths of *zempoalzúchitls,* to be rewarded for his conduct on Earth.

Xochiquétzal, on the other hand, brooded in silence when the order came from the paternal god. Above all things she loved the beauty of tender newborn plants; she was captivated by the wanton half moon of earthly love that bathes naked by night in the springs and *almoloyas* of Anáhuac. She imagined with delight the moments she would spend on Earth, looking forward eagerly to meeting handsome warriors—but she trembled to think that perhaps she would not be able to resist the temptation of living always among the mortals. Her sin would be cruelly punished by Tonacatecuhtli. The lord's will was supreme: no one would dare to go against him. He ordered Yáotl the jester to accompany the young gods with his two faces, male and female. With an entourage of *tlaloques* assembled to serenade the departure of the handsome brother and sister, the god gave the signal for them to go.

Xochiquétzal—Flowerbird—took her earthly form from the bud of a summer rose. Little by little the flower became a woman. From its petals emerged head, hair, shoulders, breasts and *nányotl;* the green leaves and stem became the back, belly and slender brown legs of a princess. Being unclothed, Xochiquétzal quickly found shelter from a tree; with lianas and ceiba leaves she fashioned herself a dress that would be the envy of all the women of Anáhuac. As she bathed her feet in the cool waters of a stream, the pebbles sang her a song of welcome.

Xochiquétzal saw her reflection in the watery mirror. She had the very finest features: her eyes were like ripe black berries; her hair as thick and silky as a field of tender grass; her mouth was small and sensual, her body brown and lissome as the autumn wind, and her legs slender as the long tail of the quétzal bird. Suddenly, next to her own reflection, the goddess saw the handsome features of a young man. Startled, she turned around, but herculean arms, encircled by bracelets of gold and tiger skin, held her fast. "Who are you, fair maid, that makes the water stop its flow to reflect your beauty?"

"And who are you, youth, who dares to interrupt my reverie?"

"I am Copilli, son of Axayácatl, disciple of Tenoch, of Tláloc and of Quetzalcóatl, Eagle Knight and Tiger Knight, lord of all the fields that you can see from the top of that rock and of the animals, streams, flowers and fruits that they contain. I have so many *macehuales* that the strands of your hair would not suffice to count them, and the many bloodstains on my buckler mark the foes I have slain: they cover my shield and even my mace . . . Can you not perceive on my forehead the emblem of the royal crown?"

Xochiquétzal, enchanted by the young Aztec's speech and bearing, was admiring Copilli's virile torso, imagining what a pleasure it would be to have him as her husband, when the female mask of the hunchback Yáotl whispered in her ear, "What a handsome youth, is he not, Princess? His shoulders are as strong as the crests of the volcano, and his shield bears the marks of his valor . . ."

Xochiquétzal remembered her duty as goddess: she must not succumb to the temptations of mortal love. But the jester's words increased her admiration for the splendid prince, and she thought to herself, *I have brought love to so many mortals when they have asked me through the burning* copal *of their censers. But now I myself am alone, without a mate, condemned to look upon warriors and nobles and to shun the touch of their hands and lips.*

"What are you thinking about, maid?" interrupted Copilli, who had neither seen nor heard Yáotl.

"That the eyes of the *océlotl* whose jaws crown your head shine like the twinkling Citlaltonac."

"No more than your own, woman, which are like obsidian sequins or censers of burning jade."

In silence they gazed at each other for a few moments. Then the prince said, "I asked you who you were. I do not know you. Judging by your alien costume, you must be from a foreign land."

"I am indeed, O Prince: I am the daughter not of one of your servants or *macehuales* but of a king more powerful than you and your father, whose voice is obeyed and worshipped by the very clouds, the sun, the maize and the water."

"Where is this king so mighty that he must be the wonder of his lands? Why has he not come to render tribute to my father? You must know that the Aztec race is master of the whole world, even that which lies beyond the mountains and the sea."

"My kingdom lies yet farther away."

"But I rule even as far as Huehuetlapallan and Chicomóstoc."

"My kingdom lies yet farther away."

"My father's warriors have vanquished the Olmec-Uixtotin and the Cuextec tribes."

"I come from still farther beyond."

"Beyond those lands there is nothing save the clouds and the rainbow, the fields of white deer and downy hummingbirds. Beyond those lands there is only the dwelling place of the good and evil gods, the Omeyocán and Tamoanchán—the land of paradise."

"It is as you have said."

"And why, then, instead of this body, are you not like a transparent breeze or like the warble of gray partridges, or the perfume of violets or the crystal flow of water in this stream?"

"That is a mystery which only the gods know."

Copilli laughed, mocking laughter, more calculated than incredulous. He had never seen a young woman like this one. Not even in drawings on the deerskins that adorned the walls of the royal palace could such an image be seen. The prince heard desire in the hummingbird's song. "Come," he said, taking the hand of the exquisite young maid.

She allowed him to lead her, as the *océlotl* is led to the pool by tracks of deer, there to kill them. She walked with a godlike serenity and in her movement Copilli saw the gentle swaying of roses in the spring breeze.

They walked in silence. With the touch of the prince's hand Xochiquétzal had become more and more human: she was ready to offer herself to him. A voice within her head reminded her of her celestial origin—her duties, the point of her existence.

Copilli's country villa was a spacious dwelling of stone and adobe, with a solemn and majestic air. At the door two warriors stood guard; there were others nearby, resting or playing. Some were feeding the wild animals that had been caught on the prince's latest hunting expedition and were kept in stout straw cages.

The arrival of the couple interrupted the activities of the Aztec officers and the servants; the lovely stranger attracted many glances.

"This is my house," Copilli murmured in her ear, "From now on, its walls will be yours as well. The fire in the hearth will warm your body and cook your meals. My servants will attend to your comfort and repose. My jesters will make you laugh. My warriors will be your escort. My name will safeguard your life, as the river stone shelters the white fish."

Without a word Xochiquétzal crossed the threshold. The coals of a slow fire sweetened with *copal* filled the room with a fragrant odor and provided a comfortable warmth. The walls were hung with weapons and trophies won in hunting and war. Skins of tigers, puma and deer carpeted the floor. Several *icpallis* of wicker and the finest leather seemed to grow like cornstalks inside the room. In one corner was a buried clay jug of fresh, cool agave juice. Over the hearth an enormous sheepskin painted with vegetable dyes and cochineal displayed the prince's shield: the royal crown.

"How inviting," said Xochiquétzal and, matching deed to

thought, she stretched out beside the hearth on a puma skin. Copilli watched her from above by the flickering firelight while the flames made her eyes a play of shadows and gave her smile an intriguing seductiveness.

IN TENOCHTITLÁN the prince's prolonged absence had begun to be noticed, for he had been on vacation since his anointment as a *tecuhtli*. No hunt, no matter how exciting, could amuse the prince for long, and in this case a whole moon had gone by and still Copilli did not return. Axayácatl's emissaries had informed him that a princess of rare beauty was staying with his son—though refusing to share the warmth of his bed —and was tormenting him with her denials. Upon hearing the news, the king had become concerned. Who might that woman be? An adventuress, perhaps. Or maybe a Huáxtec spy—they were known for their beautiful women—or a country maid versed in the arts of witchcraft.

The lord's meditations were interrupted several days later by the arrival of one of Copilli's messengers, breathless from running. When they had revived him with hot herbal tea, he said to the king, "Lord, I greet you in the name of your son, who charges me, first of all, to wish you peace and fulfillment in your palace and tranquillity of mind. Furthermore, considering that he must keep no secret from you, he asks your leave to bring before the court his betrothed, the beautiful Princess Xochiquétzal, whom he requests your consent to wed."

Furious, Axayácatl rose to his feet, stopping with a gesture the *macehual* who was fanning him with brilliant bird feathers. His necklaces of jade and emerald and his bracelets of gold and obsidian jangled. "What is that you say? Is he the one to decide whether he will marry? Does he not know that he is young and still lacks the necessary wisdom and stability? If this absurd idea were known in Tenochtitlán, it could be used against me."

He paced back and forth, then faced the messenger.

"Go tell him," he ordered, "that I advise and command him

to send this alien back to her country, wherever it be, and to appear before me within three days. Tell him that his obedience will pacify me, but his disloyalty will increase my just paternal wrath. Say to him also that the god Tláloc—that god for whom he professes so much love—appeared to me last night in a vision and told me to warn him that that woman can bring him nothing but misfortune."

The messenger backed out of the royal presence with lowered head, ready to fly. The message he bore to Copilli was the wrath of Axayácatl.

When the young prince learned his father's will, he felt it to be unjust. Was he not already sufficiently strong and able? Had he not been triumphant in wars and tournaments? Had he not matched his mace against the tiger's claws? Did his arrow not pierce the heart of the eagle in flight? Why, then, must he be denied the right to choose his consort? Copilli prepared to set off to Tenochtitlán to convince his father. He commanded that tents be taken down early next day and the litters made ready; he had ordered a special one to be made for Xochiquétzal.

That afternoon the prince invited his beautiful stranger to walk alone with him through the foothills of the mountains. Slowly and in silence they walked, as they had done the day they met. Arriving at the place where the young lord had first encountered the maid, he spread his *áyatl* of rich cloth upon the grass and invited Xochiquétzal to rest. On one knee, he contemplated the woman whom his father had forbidden him to take in marriage. Their eyes blazed—four black pupils, seductive. A languid, melting gaze. And the breath of love springing from lips, from two mouths that meet. They rolled upon the ground, their bodies entwined in the red glow of sunset. Copilli—muscles tense as flint knives; Xochiquétzal—yielding to the arms of this man turning her into fire and substance. The instants flew like frightened hummingbirds while Copilli, beside himself, succumbed to the wild intoxication of desire.

Then the mocking laughter of Yáotl the jester,

Tamoanchán's sardonic spy, rang out. The jeers shattered the fiber of Xochiquétzal's being. The very moment in which she triumphed as a woman, she was vanquished as a goddess. Thunder from the heavens boomed through the mountains. Cruel torrents of rain fell upon the couple; they sprang apart. Copilli, with a violent gesture, flung the girl from him, she who a moment before had been his delight.

In the water now pouring through the ravines and blackening the horizon, the prince had read the message of Tláloc, his protector. He saw anger and compassion in those thunderbolts, the gleaming eyes of the god in the flashing lightning. Soaked now, the two gazed at each other with a look far different from that they had shared earlier. Graceful as a gazelle, the dark maid stood up, trembling. Like a tiger, Copilli gathered himself. No words were spoken. He stalked aimlessly and then stopped, looking back. He saw her run among the bushes till she disappeared, to where her sin condemned her.

As Copilli lost sight of her blurred figure in the rain, he seemed to hear the bloody laughter once again and a sepulchral voice. "Who tries to touch the flower will die upon its thorns before he reaches its petals."

The deluge continued. Frightened animals ran through the jungle. Birds trembled in their nests. Wild beasts roared from their caves. Copilli walked toward his house. In but a few moments the vision was lost: the woman he had thought made for him was a fantasy, an error, a shadow.

Then the wise god Tláloc eased his despair and dispelled the storm. By the time Copilli reached his house the heavenly torrents had been replaced by his tears.

X

Hair of Corn

"NO, MY DEAR COPILLI," my father told me, "that way does not lead to happiness. Happiness is found within you, in your attitude to life. Be ever mindful of the gods and do not offend them by straying from the ordained path. In truth, I must tell you of the vision I saw in my dreams while you dallied with that woman.

"Tláloc and Quetzalcóatl," continued Axayácatl, "appeared to me as beautiful twins. While the first advised me to deny your request which your messenger would bring me, the other drew prophetic symbols on an *ámatl* scroll that depicted you as an advocate of aid and service to your people. And since Quetzalcóatl's prophecy cannot be fulfilled if you lack inner peace, I counsel you to calm your spirits and to restrain —in work or in war—that restlessness which can only hinder you. I will always be at your side to give you whatever help you need. I wish only for your good, as well you know."

"Thank you, lord and father," I replied. "Your wise words soothe me greatly. As for your last advice, I must admit that war does not attract me, although I am an honored and renowned member of your militia and a warrior by blood as well as duty.

"Not in vain," I went on, "have your artists drawn my figure upon your throne in Tepantitlán to remind the people that they have in Copilli a champion to defend them if ever necessary. But more than to war, I find myself drawn to the task— perhaps more demanding and dangerous—of studying and imparting justice and planning the future, that is, the work of a *tlacuilo*. To this art, that you yourself know so well and have shown to me, I must dedicate my life."

"You have spoken well, my son. May your spirit persevere and scale those summits that you have set as your goal. You have your father's personal esteem and King Axayácatl's support for your endeavor."

WE WERE SPEAKING in the *tecpán* of Tenochtitlán, after the unhappy incident with Xochiquétzal. In my soul, at first perplexed, the storm had cleared. I now felt a growing need to build and to act. From that day on I tried to participate in all matters, without neglecting my obligations as emperor's son before the lords and nobles. Thus I learned other languages, alien-sounding to the priests, but which enabled me to communicate with many men of diverse customs, friends of our nation. I also learned the art of the *amantécatls,* feather workers, and that of the *tlacuilos,* or artists: I produced works of esthetic merit, and, employing my second skill, I created, with other *tlacuilo* friends, a periodical codex for the delight and information of the Aztecs. Its handsome looks and beneficial purpose were widely commented upon. As I am sensitive by nature, I also composed several songs to women and to love, inspired perhaps by certain melodies of Netzahualcóyotl. Neither did I fail to make my presence felt among those who dedicated themselves to the mysterious, subtle craft that the Aztecs call the seventh art.

All these activities, however, which in an ordinary person would be cause for praise, only brought upon my head the very harshest criticisms. I was accustomed to slander, so I continued to live the life that pleased me, unaffected by attacks and insinuations. But I did not neglect to weigh my acts carefully so as not to give cause to my detractors. I knew that it would be felt that Prince Copilli had no right to be an artist or *tlacuilo,* to compose songs or anything of the sort. Like it or not, I was supposed to conform absolutely to the stereotyped image that nations develop, often unconsciously, for the children of their leaders.

My relations with girls were like those of any ordinary warrior. In the Calmecac itself we were advised to associate with many and not commit ourselves to one until the time for marriage. Despite such instructions, I never took women for animal pleasure, like the coyote capering with *itzcuintlis.* I tried to derive from my dealings with them, however difficult, the sacred essence that makes the surrender more delicious. I frequented houses of *cihuatlanquis,* women who arranged amorous encounters between youths and damsels in exchange for gold, salt and objects of jade and obsidian. Even there I tried to be different and act discreetly, never forgetting that it was a commercial operation and therefore distasteful to me. In the houses of *cihuatlanquis,* I found myself among many familiar faces: noble lords, warriors and *tlacatécatls,* regents and *cihuacóatls*. At one party I encountered the *tlacalel* himself, prime minister of the empire.

As for other maidens whom I looked upon with innocent and simple interest, I was never able to associate with them for a reasonable amount of time: with the knowledge that Copilli was interested in their daughter, the girl's parents tried to push events along, sending emissaries to my palace or my father's, so a match could be arranged as quickly as possible. Conscious of my age and my aspirations, I fled from those commitments. At that time, setting up a household would have impeded my intellectual preparation; and doing it badly would have caused unparalleled misfortune for my wife and for me.

Then one day I met Xílotl, Hair of Corn.

She was the most beautiful woman in the world. She came from far-off lands, whence the fame of her beauty had reached Anáhuac. The nobles and courtiers of Tenochtitlán society perhaps found her less worthy because she had been seen by so many eyes, exhibiting her extraordinary gifts. She arrived in our city and I was one of the last to meet her, although her litter was often to be seen in the Great Plaza, the *teocalli* and the avenue of Tlacopán, and she was fond of riding in a canoe through the canals of Xochimilco. At first I thought she was cold, soulless, incapable of giving and receiving a true and stable love, a love which I needed, together with the fulfillment of my obligations, to feel complete.

Once I saw her riding alone in a boat across a pond; after exchanging the usual greetings, we spoke briefly of insignificant matters. Her conversation was like that of any other woman—they all sound alike to a man; I thought she was calculating. Besides, I noticed that she had not taken to me. My second impression occurred one night when I had retired to my palace with my faithful attendants. In my desire for repose I had ordered that the torches be extinguished and the night round begun in silence. A strange sensation of emptiness began to invade me. When at last I managed to sleep, it was only to see Xílotl amid clouds, very different from how I had imagined her—faithful, affectionate and passionate. I awoke with the urgent need to see her.

I roused my servants. They wondered what had happened in this peaceful palace to make Copilli stride through his galleries, shouting. No one could convince me that it was pointless to go to her house at such a late hour of the night. I called together the Imperial Choir, whose sweet voices I have loved since I was a child, and with them stood beneath the arches of her dwelling, determined to delight Xílotl's dreams with old melodies of Anáhuac which she had never heard.

The demonstration did not move Hair of Corn. But spurred by passion, I continued to declare my affection with fervent insistence. It was in vain. She allowed me to accompany her but showed no signs of affection. Little by little, however, I began to penetrate her soul and accustom her to my ways. My attentions finally overwhelmed her; the assurance with which I spoke to her bewitched her. And at last her eyes shone, and she was mine.

From that time on she transformed the world for me. The miraculous change continued to work in her, perhaps thanks to Tláloc's art, for I had so often asked him for advice and strength. Her coolness had become warmth and sweetness; her wariness, sincerity. Our love left no room for jealousy. She took pains with her appearance to please only me, while I helped her to maintain her reputation as the most beautiful woman on earth. Her domestic skills impressed me. I delighted in the meals she prepared for me. She proved to be both companion and lover. She brought me spiritual peace; she helped me to feel more self-possessed.

I realized now that I should be less ambitious with regard to my future role in the life of the empire, and that I should concern myself with my own life, which I had been impeded from developing fully. I decided to retire forever from public view and public censure, away from those Aztecs whom I loved so dearly. At the same time, I recognized a duty not to go without leaving them in writing my ideas concerning the nation's government and well-being, thoughts inspired by the

wise counsel of Axayácatl and in the predictions of Tláloc and
Quetzalcóatl.

THIS THEN is the reason for this hieroglyphic pyramid. This
the reason that I know myself and that I leave—to those who
can appreciate it—a comment upon the era in which I lived so
close to the *icpalli*. Now I am content in the company of my
wife.

YOU, MOXOTLI, now you are to continue reading the history of
Anáhuac on the walls of this prodigious monument. . . .

XI
The Second Moctezuma

Moxotli continued his narration:

"SOME TIME after King Chalchiutlanetzin took the oath in Tollán and before the supreme council was dissolved, a law was established with the mutual accord of king and populace: no king could reign for more than two *tlalpillis*—knots or cycles—of years as they were measured then, that is, six of our years. If the king were to die before finishing his term, judges appointed by the people would govern for the time that remained. When the six years were over, the king must pass on his throne to another, chosen by the gods. This successor would reign independent of the former king, who was obliged to withdraw from government for the rest of his life.

"No Aztec historian has indicated exactly why this law was established. It is known that there was a need for it, a situation that cost blood and many lives, especially during the lifetime of the judicious Hueman, whose leadership had so pleased and satisfied the people and whose words were revered as if they were sacred. In a later era they passed another law that stipulated that any lord—whatever his realm or chiefdom— who showed a certain ambition or desire for power before the suitable time for selection of the king's successor would be excluded from consideration and rejected by his subjects. It is not unreasonable to suppose that in order to guard against abuses, this law was instituted by the wise Toltecs, the first and oldest lawmakers in the world.

"Like other lords, your father, the first *tecuhtli* who did not belong to the military caste, strengthened the order of the three branches, trying to bring about a balance between the people and the army. At the end of his fifth year, he began a period of penance; he needed to commune with the Tamoanchán, asking for counsel and inspiration from the very *Tloque Nahuaque* himself.

"For thirteen months—sixty days long at that time—he must do penance in the splendid Temple of the Locust, which stood, surrounded by pine trees, at the very entrance to the Cincalco. From the temple the thirteen heavens could be contemplated, very similar to the Temple of the Frog.

"The king began his penance by painting his body black. During the entire period he had to maintain a strict fast, except on the principal feast days. He was not allowed to imbibe any sort of intoxicating drink, even on feast days; he could drink only water. The priests and *tecuhtlis* went to the temple on alternate days. They brought the finest foods they could obtain and ate them in front of the penitent lord in order to make his abstinence more painful. At the same time, they heaped opprobium upon him, and continually went from word to deed, pulling his hair, cuffing him on the neck and otherwise badgering him. Throughout all this the penitent had to remain impassive. He could not protest the insults or respond otherwise than with the most polite and restrained words. Neither was he permitted to use any force; he had to accept everything with supreme patience and humility. The populace too assaulted him with vicious words; he was almost never left in peace. Afterward he had to pass through the entire kingdom to reconsider his acts, while he was showered with petitions and requests and reminded of former promises that he had not been able to fulfill. Few were those who received him with laurel branches. At the end of this trip he was expected to address the *tecuhtlis* and then, when the sixty days were over, he would receive divine inspiration and propose the name of the chosen one.

"When that final moment was almost at hand, your father took his place upon the last step of the Temple of Huitzilopochtli, facing the altar of the idol. Standing before an enormous smoking brazier, he began to burn laurel branches in sacrifice. Then, uttering reproaches to the idols, he pierced his lips, nostrils and ears. Suddenly he heard a sound like the murmur of thousands of grasshoppers coming from the Tamoanchán: *Moctezuma . . . Moctezuma . . .*

" 'Moctezuma?' your astonished father said to himself; then his head cleared: 'Of course, Moctezuma Xocoyotzin is the man who must govern, without a doubt.'

"Then he had to determine the day he would leave the temple and communicate his choice to the nation. Before that he must tell Moctezuma himself and first, out of courtesy, he must inform the great *huey tecuhtlis* and the commander of the armies. His choice had to be announced to the commanders of the three branches so that they might propose it to the nation. This was the way to ensure continuity, so essential for the accomplishment of greater goals in Anáhuac.

"Axayácatl approached the door of the temple and walked through the gardens; the grand lords were there, but not seeing Moctezuma, he invented a pretext to send for him. When the latter arrived, Axayácatl told him simply, 'You're the one. Your name rang loudly in my ears and echoed in my brain. Suddenly my eyes saw and my heart felt the very clearest of signs. Now I will inform all those who are gathered together here, so that they may in turn let the news be known throughout the entire kingdom.'

"Moctezuma remained silent for a long time, as if in a dream, and then at last he humbly thanked the king. Axayácatl summoned two of the most important lords.

" 'Go and let it be known to all *tecuhtlis* that Moctezuma is the man,' he told them in a calm and clear voice. 'Then report to me the opinion of my kingdom.'

"A surprised murmur was heard. No voice, however, was raised in opposition. Although Moctezuma was not a young man, no one protested. They all played the game: discipline, organization, national spirit, virtues only to be found in the military organization and in war. The disappointed aspirants felt as though their hearts had been ripped from their breasts; but hiding their pain with the skill that comes with their office, they ran to congratulate the chosen of the gods.

"Your father knew what would happen to him, but that was not important. Those were the rules of the game. Soon Axayácatl's friends would repeat the insults from the period of penance—now, as they claimed, in the name of Moctezuma. And Moctezuma's friends would do the same, until they had succeeded in estranging the two. Thus they might maintain their influence with the new lord.

"Axayácatl met with Moctezuma to inform him of the matters which would become his responsibility and the honor he was about to receive. He counseled him to be humble, patient, sober and prudent so that he might better guide the nation. Before Moctezuma left, Axayácatl told him to set up residence in another house where he might receive the people's blessing and support. This he did.

"You remember that your father Axayácatl informed you beforehand so that you could go greet and congratulate Moctezuma."

"Yes, I do remember. He gave me a valuable lesson in politics. He had me wait in the Green Room of his palace so I might see and hear a group of people from his home region. They had come to see him in connection with another *tecuhtli* whom they believed would be chosen by the gods; his palace was opposite that of Axayácatl. They implored Moctezuma to intercede for them so that the *tecuhtli* would receive them and accept their unconditional support. In this way they hoped that the gods would favor their prayers. And he did: he sent a *tameme* or messenger to lead the distinguished ambassadors to the *tecuhtli*'s presence.

"As soon as they had departed, Moctezuma said to me, 'You see? That's politics . . . When they are halfway there they'll find out. . . .'

"Days before the acceptance ceremony, the capital was filled with *tecuhtlis* who would witness Moctezuma's arrival at the Temple of the Frog, where he would be received into the order of *tecuhtli*. He performed the rite: piercing his lower lip, the cartilage of his nose and his ears with bones of tigers, lions, eagles and other animals, he implored the gods to give him a lion's courage, a tiger's cunning, the strength of an eagle that flies so high and straight, and the agility of a hart. Surrounded by close friends and distant relatives, he received gifts: exquisitely wrought gold and silver pieces, many of them garnished with emeralds and other precious gems; innumerable fabrics and garments of different weaves, hues and decoration, cloth woven not only of cotton thread but also of rabbit hair, headbands and belts made of feathers of exotic colors. He was given so much that was valuable and costly, and in such abundance, that one hundred and eighty men were needed to carry the load.

"When you asked him what he was thinking of doing, he

replied, as you will remember: 'I'm going to give you another brief lesson in politics, a thought you must always remember so that no one can get the better of you: *Old men talk about what they have done and fools about what they are going to do.*'

"The three branches performed the ceremony of tribute before all the *tecuhtli* knights, rulers of different towns, judges, tribute collectors, ministers, soldiers and common people, all of them facing a stone tribune divided into three wings.

"Moctezuma delivered his address; in essence it contained what his ambassadors had already said. He was benevolent, genial and mild, yet ever decorous and circumspect. A prearranged triumphant ovation indicating delighted satisfaction burst forth when he mentioned the reconciliation of princes.

"His great march through the empire would begin shortly, and of this journey there is little to say. It has always—at least up to now—been triumphal, since the power of the *tecuhtlis* is gauged not by their wealth or prestige, but rather by their closeness and access to the emperor, and all of them of course make a great show of their friendship with him.

"The day came for the impressive ceremony of the handing over of power, which takes place, if not in the Temple of Huitzilopochtli itself, then always before his image. By that time Moctezuma's singular qualities and the talent which the gods had bestowed upon him had begun to shine forth. Some people had believed that the company of his colleagues would diminish his grandeur, but, in fact, their presence served to enhance it. They had been the first humbly to admit inferiority, and repeated over and over again that the government was entirely in his hands and that they were most happy to worship and obey him. Never had the path of a future sovereign been so free of obstacles to success. The other vassals extolled—in advance—the judicious government of their new sovereign; they felt that he possessed and even surpassed all the outstanding qualities of his predecessors put together. Axayácatl had conquered many enemy flags; now it befell the mighty Moctezuma to preserve the empire's glory.

XII
The Transfer-of-Power
Ceremony

"CAPTAIN HUITZITÓN, leader of the people of Aztlán for many years, was indefatigable, valiant and vigorous and sought always what was best for his nation. Burdened with years, he died suddenly one night. It is said that in order to diminish the pain his people might suffer in the face of such an irreparable loss, the ancients told them that he had been carried away to Tezcatlipoca, the god who sits on a frightful dragon and is thus called Tetzauhtéotl, 'terrifying god.'

"Tezcatlipoca, ordering him to sit at his left side, said, 'Welcome, brave captain. Well you deserve this seat. I am pleased with how you have served me and governed my people; it is time now for you to rest and to rise to the chorus of the gods for the many deeds you have performed. Return to your children, the *tlamacazques,* and tell them not to grieve. Although you may not be with them, you will not cease to watch, care for and govern them from the nine places, the nine heavens. Once your flesh is consumed, I will see to it that your children be given your skull and bones to console them and assuage their pain. Through these they may consult you about the path they must follow and all that concerns their government, and you will lead them.'

"Thus were the people beguiled and their grief mitigated. They began to render divine honors to Huitzitón, giving him the name Huitzilopochtli instead of his own and calling him *mapoche*—'left hand,' that was to say, 'Huitzitón seated on the left.' From then on the ancients began to rule, pretending to consult the skull on all government matters and claiming that it answered them and led them wisely. This is the origin of the famous deity to whom a huge cult paid homage through the later centuries. The nations which inhabited these regions worshipped him as god of war, and in his honor they constructed the famous Temple of Mexico, known later to the Spaniards. It is before this deity that the ceremony of the handing over of power is performed in Mexico.

"Now all was ready for the great ceremony. Not only were the *tecuhtlis* of the kingdom's capital invited once more, but also the leaders of neighboring and foreign realms. Outside the temple, the populace observed the stately passage of the kings, followed by important personages, relatives and friends. Seats for all the *tecuhtlis* had been installed in the temple. In front of each seat was the gift that each was to receive: robes and all sorts of garments; feathers, gold and silver jewels, precious stones according to their lineage and political or military rank; shields, bows, arrows and maces. (In later times, according to don Fernando de Alva Ixtlilxóchitl, the gifts included male and female slaves.)"

"THE MOMENT ARRIVES; all is ready in the temple. The old king makes a triumphal entrance. With great humility, he crosses the sacred chamber while all the *tecuhtlis* stand and applaud him. He climbs the high, narrow steps that lead to his place in the center in front of Huitzilopochtli.

"Soon a great din is heard; the new sovereign makes his entrance. Unlike the king, who has come in alone, he is surrounded by many *tecuhtlis*. Smiling, he moves forward, bowing first to one side and the other, greeting each lord. With gestures of his hands, he expresses his thanks to all. He ascends the stairs and greets the king, who, standing, awaits him. In this instant the new sovereign is another man. And the ceremony begins.

"It is important to point out that the outgoing king says nothing during the entire ceremony except for a few ritual words. He removes the new sovereign's humble vestments and dresses him in richer, finer garments embroidered with the Order of the Eagle. His hair is tied with a red ribbon with feather tassels hanging from the ends. Immediately the outgoing king places on his head a crown-shaped adornment made of the same feathers; on the front it bears a painted image of the animal or bird he wishes to reflect in bravery, strength and intelligence.

" 'Receive, lord, this symbol of the absolute power which I hand on to you and which will be yours for six years; use it well, for the benefit of the kingdom and its people.' Then, facing Huitzilopochtli, he places a bow in Moctezuma's left hand and several arrows in the right. At the same time he gives him a few grains of gold. 'Do not let my shadow obstruct the Sun: the sun must reflect your shadow alone. With these arms I hand you, you must symbolically kill me.'

"The grains of gold, together with incense, are thrown into

a brazier at the idol's side. The fire flares and a small column of smoke rises to form a small cloud smelling of *copal.* With this the temple shakes with a great roar from the throats of the *tecuhtlis.* The prolonged ovation lasts until a signal from the new sovereign. He speaks. First, an exhortation: he says that the office to which he has been elevated will not be used as a source of vanity or pride, but rather of humility, honesty, chastity and abstinence, and fruitful, creative work. In this spirit he dedicates himself to good administration and defense of the State.

"The speech lasts a long time. It contains the soundest precepts, the noblest promises. The former king listens silently, knowing that to a large extent he is being affronted and reproached. At last the new sovereign bows to the idol and the former king—and then he waves an uplifted hand, bowing from side to side as he did when he entered the temple. With this, the ceremony concludes.

"The new king, in a gesture of magnanimity (thus is royal courtesy called), invites the former monarch to his palace for the last time. He leaves the temple, adorned with all the insignia of his new power and accompanied by his retinue. To the drumming of *teponaxtlis* and *tlapahuéhuetls,* they parade through the central streets of the city, led by jesters and crude comedians who make funny faces, jokes and witticisms to amuse the populace and win their applause.

"From this day on, new *tecuhtlis* begin to enjoy privileges and exemptions, governorships, presidencies and other high-ranking positions such as collectors and distributors of tribute and honors. It is a new life. Everything starts over again. . . .

"According to Aztec tradition, the king hangs his predecessor's sign or insignia on his palace gate for six days; then, to humiliate him, he displays it for six years in one of the main rooms of the palace to which the population has free access. Thenceforth, the drama is a long spectacle of moans, sighs, tears, shouts, treason and cowardice and cheers."

XIII
The Warning

"AFTER YÁOTL THE JESTER sent Quetzalcóatl away, nothing was heard of the plumed serpent; only his predictions were remembered. It was believed that one day he would return, not as a man but as a god."

"On an afternoon of arduous labor for Moctezuma, the sovereign had retired to his palace; he was playing a game of *patolli*. He had won a few games, then retired to rest for a while. Suddenly the curtains of the antechamber swept open and a man entered. His body was painted green, his face covered by the head of a huge boa and his shoulders enclosed in rich feathers. Amazingly, on removing his sandals, he suddenly became a giant. In a soft tone, he addressed Moctezuma: 'Lord, I am Quetzalcóatl.'

"Moctezuma, frightened at first but reassured by the sweetness of the voice, replied, 'What do you want of me?'

" 'I come only to remind you,' answered Quetzalcóatl, 'that your reign is almost over. Remember that a great government consists in knowing how to curb rivalries effectively. A sovereign must hear and not hear, see and not see. He must always bear in mind the needs of the nation. A good sovereign is always better than a good law, since he who does not know how to govern is nothing more than an usurper: he has deceived his people.

" 'You should be thinking about the person who will succeed you, Moctezuma. You should consider who your true friends are, those to whom you must always listen. You must seek among your associates a young man, for your nation is also young.

" 'This person must already have held positions of high authority which have sharpened his sense of responsibility. Like you, Moctezuma, the chosen one must discover the secret of winning the nation's support by an austere and temperate life. He who governs must have authority and initiative, but not always: there is nothing more damaging to the empire than a fool who thinks he is a wise man, especially if he is going to govern for the general good. Remember that a nation's greatest need is to be governed. Bad leaders are punished by being judged worse than they really are.

" 'Many injustices have been committed in the name of other sovereigns. The most pressing need is not to make the people rich, feed them and reduce the living cost. Those are things of the moment. What is more important is to protect the people by providing them with work and thus allowing them to grow stronger by their own efforts. The greatest danger is to govern too much. It is better for the kingdom that men give rein to their vices than abuse their virtues. A government's power rests only in those who let themselves be governed. A sovereign is more easily forgiven a bad life than a long one. Those who hold the power will always invoke rule, those of the opposition, liberty. Factions can change their tendencies but never their name. Do not let your power rest too heavily upon the law: it is easier to enact a law than to apply it.

" 'This afternoon,' continued Quetzalcóatl, 'Copilli has completed his pyramid. These words of advice are written upon its four faces. You would be wise to read them and engrave them upon your mind and heart.'

"Suddenly, hearing a noise, Quetzalcóatl disappeared.

"Moctezuma's chamber attendant entered and, seeing his master, exclaimed, 'What has happened, lord? You are quite pale.'

" 'Nothing,' Moctezuma replied. 'Only what happens to all human beings. One cannot depend upon others, even if he trusts them implicitly. Our friends have forgotten us. The fifth year is very difficult; I do not even trust the gods. This is the year of the Tezcatlipoca complex. What will the last year be like, and then my first year in the Tamoanchán? May Quetzalcóatl protect me. Olmózotl, let us go to Teotihuacán.' "

XIV
The Tomb

ALL WAS READY in *Teotihuacán. Flower sacrifices had been offered in the small temple dedicated to friendship whose symbol was two intertwined arms, hands open. Women, musicians and dancers, warriors and animals entered the plaza by the main gate. The pointed, waving pole of the volador had been raised; from its top men would imitate the eagles, disturbing the clouds with the sound of their small drums.*

IT WAS MY DAY. Copilli's day. It was for this that I had brought together so many people and arranged so many amusements. In front of me, the pyramid; around me, my friends and advisers. The former had come to bid me farewell; the latter would be inscribed forever on the gigantic stones. I announced my decision to bury myself alive in the pyramid. My vision of Anáhuac obliged me to make this final sacrifice. I felt powerless to alter my resolution despite my personal wishes, my father's advice and Tláloc's divine inspiration. I was not frightened. The blood of my race seemed to course more violently through my veins. That was when Tláloc said to me, "When you enter that pyramid for the last time, the image of my consort, goddess of rain, will seal the entrance; no one and nothing will be able to remove it. Perhaps some day you will rejoin your people, following your father's example; but from this moment hence, you too have entered the Tamoanchán."

With a grateful glance I acknowledged his words. Tláloc was more than a god: for me he had been the living spirit of the Aztec race—its traditions, needs, vices and virtues—in constant dialogue with me. His divine power had protected me. His *tlaloques* had guided my steps since I was a child. Not in vain had my father Axayácatl also enjoyed the company and the advice of the Lord of Rain, Quetzalcóatl's secret emissary. I did not take my eyes from the god's visage, whom only I could see.

At that moment the scene was interrupted by a guard who ran in shouting. "Hundreds of people are coming this way, Copilli," he told me. "Your father's friends, led by the emperor, Moctezuma, are coming from Tenochtitlán. They say that they bear you a message from Quetzalcóatl."

I was afraid. I faltered. If I waited for the king, I would be abandoning my resolve. To listen to my father's friends could mean entering public life, being named *tlacatécatl, tecuhtli* or *cihuacóatl*, perhaps even aspiring to the royal crown whose name I considered more of a hindrance than a goal. I decided not to wait.

I pronounced my final instructions amid the quiet weeping of my faithful friends. I bid them farewell. They kissed my hand and made small cuts on their arms and legs to show they would shed their blood for me. In that moment, everything we had shared came back to me: studies, adventures and games, discussions of the empire, accounts of its life, acts of justice for *macehuales,* and much more. They had remained loyal to me to this moment. Well they knew that none could ever appreciate their friendship more than I.

It was getting late. "Lord," I said to Tláloc, "let rain prevent them from arriving in time." The god made a sign: seven *tlaloques* broke their pitchers over Teotihuacán. The deluge did not deter my friends and servants from forming a path for me from my tent of *océlotl* skins to the entrance of the monolith.

Turning to Xílotl, I said, "*Yolo*—dearest—you will not accompany me. You will remain here. I have no right to deprive you of something as beautiful as life." She began to weep. The rain lashed her hair—in truth as golden as ripe corn—and molded her garments to her body, making her even more lovely.

I strode quickly to the entrance, where the captain of the eagle knights stood. "*Cuauhtlitecuhtli,*" I ordered him, "shoot at anything that comes near. Do not allow anyone to try to dissuade me." With this, I turned to enter the pyramid.

I heard Xílotl cry out, "*Yolo, yolo,*" and, turning my head, I saw her running toward me, her hair streaming behind her in the storm.

My loyal eagle knight shot an arrow from his bow. My lovely Xílotl fell to the ground. No one moved.

I looked furiously at the *cuauhtlitecuhtli* captain, who seemed to answer me with his eyes, "It was you who ordered me to do it." There was nothing I could say. I ran to Xílotl, took her in my arms and from her dying lips I heard, "Yolo. . . ."

The love I bore my country and my people could not assuage the grief that I felt at that moment. My heart was torn between my nation and her memory. I sensed that in heaven, or in my other life inside the pyramid, I would find a way of life and death that would give meaning to my existence and determine my fate. I chose my own path—communication with the stars and with my people from within the pyramid. I had never wanted to be like other men, had not tried to follow my father's path, where I could not be myself. Now I would not be obliged to be better than my father, denying, attacking and forgetting him in order to become powerful and respected. Here I could be stronger being myself, simply myself. Here I could better serve my country, in humility and firmness, and honesty—beginning with being honest with myself.

I took Xílotl into the pyramid with me.

THE DOOR WAS SEALED with the huge image of the Goddess of Rain which Copilli had ordered to be carved in honor of his mother. At once the divine deluge ceased as abruptly as it had begun, leaving two raindrops imprinted on the cheeks of the stone image. Two tears.

Arriving at that moment, Moctezuma exclaimed, "Oh, Copilli, you have understood nothing. Huitzilopochtli said that sacrifices are to be made with the hearts of others, best of all with enemy hearts, but never with one's own."

IN THE COSMOS, only fantasy is real.

Glossary

THE PRONUNCIATION of Náhuatl words is not as difficult as the formidable assemblage of oddly combined consonants would suggest. The vowel sounds are like those in Spanish. Most consonants and consonant combinations likewise are similar to Spanish: *qu* is pronounced like English *k;* *hu* and *gu* are like English *w* when preceding a vowel. Unlike the Spanish, however, the Náhuatl *h* is pronounced and rather "breathy" at the end of a syllable. The *ll* is about like double *l* in English.

The approximate sound of *sh* is common in Náhuatl. When the Spanish priests and scribes began to render Náhuatl pictographs in Latin letters, they assigned the letter *x* to this *sh* sound. Thus *Mexica,* a name for the Aztec peoples, is pronounced Meh-SHEE-ka. Later Spaniards, however, gave this *x* the sound of English *h*—or Spanish *j*—as they did in their own country. (Now, compounding the error and the indignity, in Spain they tend to spell the country's name *Méjico.*)

Náhuatl's ubiquitous *tl* combination is pronounced like the same letters in English "kettle," but more sharply, with almost a click of the tongue.

The accent in Náhuatl falls on the penultimate syllable. But in Spanish the final syllable is accentuated unless it ends in a vowel or *n* or *s;* any variation from this rule requires a written accent mark to indicate the stress. Hence many Náhuatl words bear written accents in order to make the Náhuatl rule conform to the Spanish rule.

acálotl   canoe

Acapulco   community on Pacific coast south of Tenochtitlán, present-day popular resort

ácatl   reed

Acolhuacán   original home of the Alcolhuas

Acolman   village near Teotihuacán

agave   common Mexican cactus, *maguey*

ahuehuete   coniferous tree similar to cypress

Alcolhuas   neighboring central valley kingdom; Texcocans

almaloya   pool

amantécatl   craftsman; feather artist

ámatl   paper made from a tree bark

Anáhuac   lake region of Mexico's central valley

atl   water

átlatl   spear-throwing device

Atlixqueños   southern dominion foes of Tenochcas

Atzcapotzalco   home of the Tepanecas in the central valley, foes of Aztecs

Axayácatl   Aztec emperor; Copilli's father

áyatl   fabric cloak or robe

Aztlán   place of origin of the Mexica

cacomixtle   badgerlike nocturnal animal

Calmecac   college wherein young men prepared for military careers

calpulli   quarter, or territorial entity, the common property of a number of families

calzontzín   absolute monarch

capulín   fruit resembling black cherry

cauhtli   eagle

ce ácatl   "one reed," a calendar date

centli   cornstalk

cetécpatl   flint

Chalcas   another lake-region tribe, enemies of Tenochtitlán

chalchiupétlatl   bejeweled tapestry

Chalchiutlanetzin   ancient king of the Toltecs

Chalchiutlicue   Tláloc's companion; goddess of sweet water

chapópotl   the "marvelous water . . . dark liquid" (oil)

Chapultépetl   a suburb west of Tenochtitlán; present-day Chapultepec Park of Mexico City

Chichimec   general term for various Nahua-speaking tribes of central Mexico

Chicomecóatl   "Seven Snake"; goddess of crops, maize

Chicomóstoc   after Aztlán, original dwelling of Aztec tribe

chimalli   shield

Chimalpopoca   early Tenochca ruler, imprisoned and murdered by rival, Maxtla

cihuacóatl   supreme magistrate with power equalling the sovereign's

cihuatlanqui   marriage go-between; procurer

Cincalco   "House of Maize"

cipactli   mythological monster

Citlaltonac   "Star That Illumines All Things"

Coatlán   temple built by Axayácatl

Coatlicue "Lady of the Serpent Skirts"; powerful goddess, mother of Huitzilopochtli

copal resin burned for incense in religious rites

copilli royal crown

Coyolxauhqui moon goddess

Cuauhnáhuac kingdom in valley south of lake area; present-day Cuernavaca

cuauhololli mace, stone-studded club

cuauhtli eagle

cuauhtlitecuhtli eagle knight—high military order

Ehécatl wind god

etzacualiztli festival honoring Chalchiutlicue

Huauxyacac a southern kingdom

huehue old man

huéhuetl vertical cylindrical drum with skin head

Huehuetlapallán place of origin of Toltec peoples

Huejotzingas southern kingdom of enemies of Tenochcas

Hueman early Aztec ruler

huey tecuhtli supreme ruler

Huitzilíhuitl early Toltec king

Huitzilopochtli major Nahua divinity; war god; also personification of noonday sun

ichcahuipilli armor of cotton-padded fabric

icpalli thronelike chair of wicker and wood; symbol of power

inezahualcalli area in the shrine for penance and dining

itácatl rucksack of provisions

itzcuintli small, hairless, edible breed of dog

Ixcóatl a king of Tenochtitlán, allied Texcocans and others to oppose Tepanecas

Ixtaccíhuatl one of Tenochtitlán's snowcapped volcanoes

Ixtlilxóchitl Texcocan chieftain, father of Netzahualcóyotl

Ixtlilxóchitl, don Fernando de Alva mestizo historian of the Conquest and of the Chichimec tribes

Janitzio island in Lake Pázcuaro, in present state of Michoacán

macehuales "people"; used to mean commoners

maguey   common agave cactus, formerly source of fibers for paper and fabric, and still source of *pulque*

malácatl   gem ornaments

mapoche   left; left hand (position of honor)

máxtlatl   breechclout

mecochiliztli   the set moon

meztli   moon; month

Mexica   one of the names of the Aztec people

mextozoliztli   the risen moon

Mictlantecutli   god of hell and death

Mixcóatl   early Nahua chieftain

miztli   lion (i.e., puma or cougar)

miztlitecuhtli   lion knight

Moctezuma Ilhuicamina   the first Moctezuma, emperor of the Tenochcas

Moctezuma Xocoyotzin   the second Moctezuma, also emperor of the Tenochcas; victim of Hernán Cortés and the Conquistadores

Moxotli   Copilli's artist-scribe who could "read" hieroglyphics

Nahua   Náhuatl

Náhuatl   an individual, or the language, of any of the various tribes of ancient origin who ranged from mid-Mexico down into Central America; includes the Aztecs

nányotl   womb

Netzahualcóyotl   illustrious poet-king of Texcoco

Netzahualpilli   Texcocan ruler, son of Netzahualcóyotl

neutle   *pulque*, fermented cactus-sap drink

nopal tenochoca   the *nopal* or prickly pear cactus which, beneath the eagle with a snake in its mouth, formed the symbol of the Aztecs—and present-day Mexico; one theory says that the name Tenochcas came from this word

océlotl   tiger (i.e., ocelot or jaguar)

Omeácatl   early Chichimec ruler

Omeyocán   abode of evil gods

otómitl   military leader of high rank

pantli   flag, pennon

patolli Parcheesi-like board game played with "dice" (beans marked with a certain number of pips)

Pátzcuaro lake and environs west of Tenochtitlán, in present-day state of Michoacán

pedernal flint

petate reed sleeping mat

pirul tree of Central America *(Schinus molle)*

pochtecas merchants

Popocatépetl one of Tenochtitlán's two great volcanoes

pulque fiery alcoholic drink made from *maguey* sap

Purépecha referring to Tangantzuan's people; Tarascans of Michoacán

quáchic valiant warrior; military chief

quetzal beautiful Central and South American bird with green-gold and scarlet plumage and brilliant, long tail feathers

Quetzalcóatl major Nahua diety, "Plumed Serpent"; also name of certain historical rulers

quetzalpétlat tapestry of feathers

Tacuba nearby kingdom allied with Tenochtitlán

tamemes bearers who carried loads via head straps

Tamoanchán paradise of the gods; supposedly place of origin of the Aztecs

Tangantzuan Caltzonzín Tariácuri king who slew Omeácatl and ruled over Tzintzuntzan

taparrabientos chilpayates young children

Tariácuri early tribe to west of central valley, present-day Michoacán

tecpan palace; nobleman's home

técpatl flint knife

tecuhtli dignitary or lord; term applies to upper level of ruling class; also often to gods

tecuhtlitonalpouqui seer; chief astrologer

Tehuantépetl southern city-state; present-day Tehuantepec

Telpochcalli elementary school for military and religious instruction

Telpuchtlato director of the Telpochcalli

Tenoch early Aztec leader, (possibly back formation from *tenochtli* or *tenochoca*)

Tenochcas the Mexica, Aztecs

tenochtli *nopal,* prickly pear cactus

tenochoca *nopal*

Tenochtitlán Aztec capital, on an island in what used to be Lake Texcoco, connected to mainland by causeways; heart of present-day Mexico City

teocalli temple

teocuitlapétlat tapestry woven with gold

teómetl *pulque*

teopixque priest

teotecuhtli high priest

Teotihuacán "Place of the Gods"; the ancient ruins northeast of present-day Mexico City

Tepanecas Atzcapotzalcan peoples, foes of Tenochcas

teponaxtli large horizontal wooden drum, often carved in animal shapes

tepuztocalli lance

tequihua title given a warrior who had taken or killed four of the enemy

Tetzauhtéotl the "Terrifying God"; another name for Tezcatlipoca

Texcoco neighboring kingdom and sometime ally of Aztecs; Alcolhua

Tezcatlipoca major Nahua divinity; "God of the Night Sky"; Copilli's nemesis

Tezozómoc tyrant of Atzcapotzalco

tiachcauh leader who gave arms training in the Telpochcalli

tícitl sorceress; medicine woman

tlacalel prime minister of Tenochcan empire

tlacatécatl primary military commander

tlacateco area dedicated to the god Huitzilopochtli

Tlacopán Tacuba

Tlacopanos Tacubans; sometime allies with Tenochtitlán against Tepanecas

tlacuilo painter-scribe

Tláloc   major Nahua deity; "God of Rain"; Copilli's protector

Tlalocán   earthly paradise for the chosen of Tláloc, where the drowned come together

Tlalocantecuhtli   in the beginning, succeeded Tezcatlipoca as the Sun

tlaloques   minor rain gods, minions of Tláloc

tlalpilli   period of time; e.g., 13-year period of Aztec 52-year cycle

tlalpiloni   head adornment

Tlaltecuhtli   god of Earth

Tlaltelolco   neighboring dominion of Tenochtitlán in Lake Texcoco; conquered by the Tenochcas eventually

tlamacazcalco   temple

tlamacazques   the Aztec people; "those who make offerings to the gods"

tlapahuéhuetls   huge ceremonial drum, played vertically

Tlatlauhqui Tezcatlipoca   the red Tezcatlipoca, one of the four sons of Tonacatecuhtli and Tonacacíhuatl

tlatocán   council body which nominated new emperor

Tlillán Tlapallán   eastern seashore site; probably in Maya country

tlocohtli   darts

Tloque Nahuaque   supreme deity; "he who is close to all things"

tobeyos   community peoples

tochtli   rabbit; associated with *pulque*

Tollan   old name of Tula, center of ancient Toltec culture

toloache   plant with medicinal and narcotic properties

Tonacacíhuatl and Tonacatecutli   earliest and supreme parental gods; "Our Lord and Lady of Subsistence"

tonalpouhqui   seer; astrologer; consulted on birth of child

Tonatiuh   major divinity; sun god

Tzollinco   "suburb" of Tenochtitlán

tzompantli   huge rack holding the skulls of sacrificial victims

tzin   hieroglyphic symbol denoting high rank

Tzintzuntzan   kingdom in Pátzcuaro area

volador, **pole of the**   high pole on top of which a movable platform was socketed; men dressed as gods or birds were fastened by ropes wound around the pole, and when they leaped off into space the unwinding rope rotated the platform and gave the effect of flight to the circling performers

xicapoyas   sacred water springs

xíhuitl   the new grass; a "year"

Xílotl   Hair of Corn, Copilli's love

xochimécatl   variety of flower

Xochiquétzal   "Flowerbird"; goddess; spirit of youth

Xólotl   Copilli's attendant

yaomachtl   military exercises

Yáotl   the buffoon; alter ego of Tezcatlipoca

yaoyizque   warrior

Yayauhqui Tezcatlipoca   the black Tezcatlipoca, one of the four sons of Tonacatecuhtli and Tonacacíhuatl

Ypana-Huitzilopochtli   Huitzilopochtli the Exalted

Zapotec   southern kingdom feuding with Mixtecas

zempoalzúchitl   brilliant yellow or orange flower of aster family (*Tagetes erecta*)

zenzontl   mockingbird